ANAMNESIS

Zorina Alliata

Anamnesis

CANTO I

At 3:00 PM on Friday, the NASDAQ fell shamelessly to its lowest level in years. For no visible reason at all, it just lost hope and let itself down like a tired old woman who could not pretend she's forty anymore. The Dow immediately followed it downward like a hopeless lover. Everyone on CNN could catch a glimpse of the ugly, sagging, depleted reality that had crept out in the open. A deep-felt, hurtful sigh rose from Times Square and spread all the way to Gaithersburg, MD where it reached Dante's cubicle just as he was fiddling with his fingers.

Dante, who had been following the markets every minute of the day not out of interest but rather out of excruciating boredom, stood still and observed the moment. Somewhere in the dark labyrinth of cubicles and cabinets on the second floor, there was a record of his retirement fund; just as of 3:00PM on Friday, it had fallen to about $0.70 in value. By all and any standards, his financial future did not look too bright. And yet, Dante could not find it in himself to give a damn.

He had been working for the Company for what felt like about three hundred years now. An international and, who knows, maybe interplanetary conglomerate, the Company had no physical products to sell; instead, it was selling concepts, abstracts, paradigms, clichés, the Glass Bead Game series, various responses to life's challenges, and even en-gross singular, disparate thoughts on given themes. Some of the cheaper products came free with a bottle of Red Romance wine.

Dante was employed in the Non-Negations wing of the Company. His department was created to contribute to the Future, by the way of the Improbable and the Impossible - the names of its two main divisions. A natural-born computer geek and proud of it, Dante was toiling in the lowest ranks of the Improbable; his dream, modest like his ambition, was to be promoted to the Impossible.

In the realm of the Improbable, "working" was a relative term. Dante's work was insignificant and, most of the times, useless. If sometimes he actually wrote one line of code, there were several layers of configuration managers, testing managers, integration managers, business managers, lawyers, presidents and kings, who immediately took ownership of that line of code; corrected it; documented it; saved it in several secret databases; tracked it; labeled it; had long meetings about it; and most of the times decided it harms at least some subset of the Company's interests. Even when his work was hesitantly allowed go to the next, Probable level, by that time it was weak, dry-cleaned, castrated, stripped of any trace of innovation, creativity or quirkiness that might have shown that it originated specifically in Dante's brain.

He was feeling particularly numb that Friday. It had been an uneventful week in an uneventful month in an uneventful year in an uneventful lifetime. He would have called in sick, but his boss was onto him; Dante had taken all the possible sick days, personal days and floating vacation days he could take the whole year, and it was barely April. His boss, too afraid of people to provoke an open discussion about it, had sent him a memo stating the company policies regarding "abuse" of the company-paid free time. Dante did not want to lose his job. He didn't think that anyone else would have hired him.

Even the Company Eye corporate software had some sort of hardware hiccups and had been taken off-line for maintenance. Most days, Dante would at least take some guilty pleasure in over-using or straight hacking into the Company Eye; it was a monitoring program for employees and it sometimes offered some lame fun, exposing co-workers and their pathetic hobbies, passions or emotions. It also provided him with some kind of big-picture view of the Company's intrinsic structure, otherwise as hard to figure out as life itself. One time, for example, he had found out that the Extreme Genius and the Extreme Idiot departments had the same phone number and email address.

In the pile of deceptive norms, procedures, color codes and explanatory notes that the Company administrative machine was requiring lately, the Company Eye was a raw, honest program. It was meant to look you in the eye from a corner of your screen, record every keystroke and screen shot you used, and report it to your supervisor. There was no mercy, no exception and no disillusion about its purpose. As much as he hated the idea of being watched, Dante at least appreciated being watched openly.

"This surveillance is worse than communism", Anna had once told him, in that outraged low voice she used to get when talking about the regime she grew up in and hated. But Dante did not really mind the Company Eye. It came with the job, along with his long line of nameless supervisors and other things he could not control. Dante didn't feel he had much to hide anyway; being spied on at least lent him a fake sentiment of some importance and weight.

The sudden drop in the market, still there at 3:30 PM, prompted unusual activity levels on the Company's computers. Just in time, the Company Eye popped back up on the screen, fresh from having been repaired. It coldly recorded employees as they were scrambling to sell stock on E-Trade and contact their brokers. The email volume grew 400% and the work volume, lingering around 1% all week, hit a clean 0.

Dante stretched his legs under the uncomfortable desk. He gave some thought to another trip to the kitchen for yet another cup of coffee, but his backside had found quite a convenient position in the chair and it didn't feel like moving. Besides, since his former cubicle-mate Eric had left, Dante was trying to take his good advice and drink less coffee in the afternoons.

Not that he had nothing to do; in the last two months, after the new management took over the Company, the paperwork had increased ten times. He had to fill out reports every hour and send them to his supervisor, detailing exactly what he did since the last one. He had to fill out paper forms and then enter the same data manually into the electronic time sheet on his computer. He had to color-code a long, confusing Excel sheet he never quite understood. He had to sign his name on the Department sheet, the Company sheet, the Management sheet and the Engineering sheet. He had to take responsibilities for things he had never heard of, but which were mysteriously appearing as tasks assigned to him only to disappear in the next few minutes. There was no cheating possible either; his supervisor would immediately email him if he didn't complete one of his Improbable duties.

At 4:00 PM, another memo from the senior management arrived with a crystalline sound in his Inbox. Since the new CEO had taken over, they were sending several urgent memos a day, mostly about the importance of saving 1 cent a minute by using a certain conference call option; about the absolute ban on Company-sponsored lunches during long meetings; about the strong reinforcement of a specific provision in the Company's Code of Conduct – such as wearing see-through blouses at work; detailing with sadistic pleasure the punishments a bad worker had received; announcing at great lengths who got fired that day.

In the last few days, all the memos had been about the upcoming shareholders meeting, the first one the Company was to hold since it had started the process of becoming a public firm. The executives were all very excited about the soon-to-be IPO offering and Dante could understand why – they were all going to make millions of dollars in stock. With a sigh, Dante opened the email.

"*Dear Shareholders*", it started. So now they're calling us all shareholders, thought Dante with a sarcastic smile. It must be their way of getting the employees working even harder, in the hope that the IPO of the company will bring them a few shares too.

"*The Speakers list has been changed by Mr. Rex, Vice-President of Voice and Sound. Please be informed that the following speakers will NOT be able to attend:*", continued the memo.

"*Joachimo Bellincione*"

"*Jason Cacciaguida*"
"*Christian Portinari- -Guelph*"

Dante's mouth opened large, in shock. He remained in his chair, motionless. He did not know what to think. He was not even sure he was supposed to think. Just as he was trying to find justifications and explanations, Dante also felt a mix of anger and forgotten emotions hitting him like a fist in the gut; hot, cold, awakening and painful at the same time.

Right there, at the bottom of the speakers list, Dante had read his missing father's name.

*_*_*

My family's secret, heavy obsession is longevity. I believe it had started in 1600s, with my great-great-great-great uncle. He was an important man you might read about in today's history books, back home in Romania; he did some good things, and some silly things; he was brave and strong, and yet he couldn't resist a pretty lady's looks.

I am not sure how he began his discoveries; many stories are left untold in my family. We value secrecy and never let strangers see our real nature; we smile and we lie and we don't give answers; family gatherings are sheer displays of our newest conquests of non-truths and neat speech tricks to avoid and deceive. The only thing we give out openly, truthfully, proudly, is our age.

There hasn't been one death in my family since I was born, 33 years ago. Everybody is alive, grandparents, uncles and aunts. They all come together a couple of times a year and we take the same picture of the same smiling crowd. I am the last child born in the family; my parents are still holders of the honors and positions conferred by the miracle of my birth.

Long ago, my great-great-great-great uncle found a way to override Nature's cruel moods and blind strokes; to avoid being the "1 in 3" sick people - to avoid being a bad statistic. He was a passionate mathematician and he knew how to re-arrange the numbers; re-shuffle them to spell reversible paths; re-create and re-born new, strong numbers out of diseased and weak ones. I suspect that this is how he got started, by understanding the numbers; and then, by seeing them in broad day light all around him, controlling and confounding the Nature; and then, by illuminating his way slowly through their patterns, careful, sly, making mistakes and achieving knowledge.

He discovered the 2-2-9 combination when he was 42; a rare, hidden pattern he found in the dense, sudden fogs forming at the foot of the Carpathians. It was one of the few ancient spells left over in our world; very hard to see even with an experienced eye, it only lived in the shadow, in the dust, in the silent wind. Down in the cities, Nature was fighting with people; but there in the woods, in the fog, Nature was tender, timeless and undisturbed; it had a soft core, exposed and vulnerable, and it was willing to listen to a plea.

I don't know how he happened to be there that day, if he was traveling with his royal entourage from Bucharest to Iasi; I don't know what he was wearing, if he had a beard or not; the only picture of him I have ever seen, the one I found in the history books, is an approximate portrait in dull colors. But I know how he felt when he saw the pattern; I saw it in his memories and I know the excitement, the power, the enlightenment. We have all longed for that feeling all our lives; for a moment of peace and silence when you don't have to face the horrible noise of your body aging, the disgusting taste of your own cells dying on your tongue; when time disappears or just doesn't matter - when you're one with time.

It was not only the shadowed numbers that he saw; it was also their size, the way they were positioned in contrast to each other, how they shared a bemused communication channel, a familiar link. It was harmony to be learned from there; happiness, or at least contentment; a new angle to look at life and love.

My great-great-great-great uncle was not greedy. It didn't cross his mind to play the numbers to gain wealth; besides, he was already wealthy and powerful. However,

he had his weaknesses like everybody else; I know that
he, at some point, abused the pattern. It could have been
with his numerous mistresses; love renders itself
beautifully to games of all sorts. It could have been that
he asked too much of his physical body, too often; that
the immortality he was achieving during the day paid for
his nights of orgy; that maybe once or twice, in the swirl
of passion, he got the numbers wrong.

His hands failed him first, two weeks before his horrible
death. He could not feel anything through his palms, be
it a soft skin or a burning wood; by evening, his arms
joined the non-existence and hung heavily, immobile,
from his shoulders. He should have stopped right then
and re-analyze his algorithms; re-order the theorems and
re-state the axioms; re-define his terms. But he did not
realize that it was not a mere disease, but Nature coming
to reclaim what was rightfully hers. He did not know
who the enemy was at that time; a week later, when the
royal doctor was preparing to cut away parts of his body
in order to save his life, he finally understood the
magnitude of the battle he was carrying.

He did not have any children of his own, so from his
deathbed he called in his brother and, with a rugged
voice, shared his precious knowledge. There is nothing
in writing, he said. There was no time for that and, until
then, he had never taken his gift seriously enough to
believe it needed a legacy. But there was truth in the
numbers around him; he could clearly see the sign of

death in the patterns in his room, and the number of minutes he had left before transcending into the other, numberless dimensions.

My great-great-great-great uncle did not leave a lot of knowledge, but he left enough to get his brother started. It took a few generations to figure out four more hidden patterns of great use; to ease up the task of maneuvering the numbers into small pleasures; to keep Nature increasingly at bay.

"Well, Anna, if this story wasn't so morbid, it would be kind of erotic", Lou commented, getting up from the couch. "I wish I knew how your old uncle partied all night long with a bunch of beautiful young women."

"That art was lost on us too", I said. "Nobody in my family inherited his joy for life. In fact, being boring is a great way to drop off the radar and stay alive."

Lou walked to the kitchen, carrying the teacups and the empty cookie platter. It was evening in Gaithersburg and outside the window of my condo, the mystery of the night snuck in, painting fast, dark strings of numbers into the air.

--*

Dante's manager had been appointed Chief of Nothingness a few months earlier. In the introductory

meeting set in the Conference Room 4-125, he had
showed up late and confused, had mumbled a few
Thanks to unknown senior managers, and then had lied
to all employees when he said his door will always be
open. Shortly after, the door from his office firmly
closed from the inside, never to be open again.
Preserving the Nothingness did not involve people or
work; it actually involved keeping them away for as long
as possible.

From time to time, the Chief would send a solemn,
serious email that said Nothing; it was a reminder of his
important task and authority; the email was immediately
re-sent to everyone by Dante's supervisor du jour, whose
job was to explain the Chief's message and to add
targeted, personalized Non-Meaning to it. His new
supervisor, a hairless, pretty man with bright-white
shirts, was perpetually unhappy and popping pills from
an unmarked bottle. He had taken the job straight out of
the Logical Business School and the Improbable
workplace proved to be a very bad fit. His problem was
that he was trying to see the big picture; to understand
the Company; to discover the hidden corporate ladder,
while doing his job correctly and timely. That was just
the wrong premise. Dante could have told him that the
Company was a live, breathing cosmic organism with an
evolution path so complex that only the gods might have
caught a glimpse of its whole organizational diagram;
that Logic was only one of its myriad departments and

definitely not a universally accepted answer in the upper management circles.

Dante did not have much respect for either his supervisor or his manager; but then, he did not have much respect for the human race in general. He had grown very isolated from the rest of the world, he suddenly realized. He had lost contact with old friends and never made new ones; had seen no reason to seek other people's company; had became so accustomed to avoiding adoring women, he had never given them a second look. But that Friday evening, well after closing hours, Dante was overwhelmed by a desperate desire for a friend.

He needed someone to talk to about the email he had intercepted; to speculate about the possibilities; to discuss his alternatives; he needed someone to explain himself to, to apologize for the years of neglect of the others. But mostly, he needed someone to talk to about his father.

Dante did not remember him at all; he was less than a year old when his father decided to get the heck out of there and set upon a new life. Dante had seen only one picture of the man, shown to him by a distant cousin who came to visit them when Dante was about 16. His father was very handsome, very tall and very well dressed in the picture. He was sitting at a long table, and smiling to the camera while his hand was protectively holding his wife's shoulders. His eyes seemed honest and clear. Dante had looked at the picture for a long time, hoping to see the signs of booze abuse and the cigarette butts around his father – hoping for an explanation as simple as that -, but could not find any.

He didn't think about his father much; but then he didn't think about anything too much. He had no special inclination towards philosophy or speculation; he did not miss things he did not have and did not fantasize about what could have been. Still, as soon as he saw his father's name in that Company memo, something cracked open inside of him. He could almost hear the noise. Dante had a feeling.

It was more than simple curiosity; it was a tight bunch of long-forgotten emotions and memories; the smell of fresh water at the pool when he was watching his school's father-and-son contest, alone; the tears of his mother over old letters, when she thought she was alone; the longing after his uncle's arms that hot summer at the farm, when his cousins were getting bear hugs from their father. And rising more strongly every minute for the first time in his apathetic life, Dante felt the anger.

He realized he hates his father with all his soul; but in the same time, he realized that his father had grown inside him to biblical proportions, untouchable and cold like the stone statue of the Commander. His anger had been like the Schrödinger's kitten: it never existed until Dante actually saw it.

Feeling trapped, helpless and somehow guilty in his cubicle, Dante looked again at the memo. In a company with millions of employees, Dante realized that he only knew four people: his supervisor, his manager, Anna and Eric - whom he lost touch with some time ago. Everybody else around him was just a face with no name whom he'd greet every morning, avoiding their eyes. He had never talked or met with anyone outside of the Non-Negations department. For Heaven's sake, he didn't even know his cubicle neighbor's name.

"What's your name?" he yelled suddenly, jumping up and looking over the cubicle wall. "What's your name?"

A frightened swooshing noise came from the semi-darkness in the other cubicle; fast-paced, syncopated steps hurried out. For all Dante could tell, his neighbor could have been a big rat who had learned how to type.

Falling back in his chair, he weighed his options; it was imperative that he took some kind of action, as much as his inertia and disgust with people were telling him to stay put. But there were old, strong feelings inside him that he couldn't quite control; he had found a new drive- a motivation he had not felt before. He had to overcome his utter isolation; he had to learn to talk again; as much as he dreaded it, he had to communicate.

It was easy to talk with people, as far as he could remember. When he was a child, he used to go up to strangers and say 'Hi, I'm Dante. I'm four. Can you sing with me?' because he had liked singing since the day he was born. At the time, his favorite song was Rita Pavone's Chitty Chitty Bang Bang - very appealing to his discerning musical ear. Some people would actually take him up on it and start singing along; it helped that he was a cute, curly-haired little boy with an irresistibly soft gap in his cheek.

With that, Dante swallowed the rest of the coffee from the cup and stood up. He had to start somewhere – and the only lead he had so far was the secretary who had sent the infamous memo. First thing Monday morning, he was going to call her and ask her, in a harsh and decisive manner, where his father was.

--*

Officer Kampf was 43 years old, had two PhDs and a job that paid $6.56 an hour. These were the things that Officer Kampf had always had in his mind; every minute of the day, he was painfully conscious of himself, his age, his Ph.D.s and his hourly rate. He was exactly and precisely defined by these characteristics, like a simplistic drawing of a laughing God. He was nothing more and nothing else; once one knew these things about him, one knew Officer Kampf in his entirety.

Surrounded by dead silence, he stood in majesty at the upper gate of the Company's highest floor; he guarded; he protected; he observed. He had learned a lot about the air and the heat on the floor; he had learned the timing and the intensity, the direction and the speed of particles around him; he had trained himself to count the nanoseconds and the millimeters of all movements.

There were four large screens in front of him; with a delicate maneuver of the electronic machineries at his desk, Officer Kampf could get a view almost anywhere on the floors below him. But he suspected that the images were made up; there was a glow of mystique to them. It was hard to believe that all that drama was unfolding down there; that people were spending hours arguing about strategies and campaigns; that some were crying in the bathrooms, that others were touching hands in the corners; that, like rats in a cruel labyrinth, they would pass one another without seeing each other, without understanding each other. Their world seemed so clear to Officer Kampf, and yet they blindly stumbled on all obstacles and hit all walls in their chaotic, irresponsible moves.

Nobody ever came to the highest floor of the building; there was nothing there but the large conference room 30-004, which was never used. The elevators didn't run that high either, so he was even refused the entertainment of tormenting some lost yuppie who would mistakenly end up on his floor. To get to the thirtieth floor, one had to have special security clearance for the executive stairs; as far as Officer Kampf could tell, he was he only one holding such clearance.

Every morning, while slowly but determinedly stepping on each stair, 30 floors up, Officer Kampf thought about his age, his Ph.D.s and his salary. He did not think about it in anger; some ten years ago he had abandoned any scrap of feeling and chose to not feel anymore. It hadn't been a hard decision – it came naturally after he had finished his second Ph.D.; there was nothing more he wanted or cared to know about life, people, love or loss. He had let it go, all of it, easily and smoothly. He had stepped out of life's path and modestly, silently, he had moved into limbo.

And yet, in the last couple of weeks, Officer Kampf forgot to switch his buttons on the left-side monitor. The same image stood there for days and days. When he arrived in the morning, he was surprised to see it still there; he set to change it, but then mysteriously forgot about it by the time he left home. The image, black-and-white, with that electronic outer glow to it, displayed itself blatantly, unapologetically. Furthermore, it had started to follow him home.

Officer Kampf could not help watching it. He did not think of anything in particular while staring at it; or while dreaming it at night; or when it popped in his mind uninvited, as he was driving his old Toyota through Silver Spring. He could not remember when he first saw it, or what was so special about it that it would stay with him for so long. It was nothing more than a cubicle and an employee, one of the thousands Officer Kampf had monitored since he was working for the Company.

Even through the raw eye of the old camera, the employee looked young and beautiful; even through the gray static and even beyond the rough pixels, the man appeared so perfectly and evenly built that he didn't seem real; and yet, to Officer Kampf, the young man stood as the one worthy person he had seen in a long time.

Officer Kampf had taken to spending his day standing two steps behind his usual post; coincidentally, it offered a better angle to watch the left-side monitor. Every so often, his eyes would linger a bit as the young man made small moves – drinking coffee, moving papers around. He had a routine of his own and Officer Kampf took it upon himself, as innocent amusement, to figure it out. There were three coffee breaks a day, at 9:00 AM, 11:30 AM and 3:00 PM. There was small chatter with a lady friend, whom for some reason Officer Kampf detested already. There was the morning reading of the Wall Street Journal, and then the confused and bored face after turning the last page. There was a lunch break, many times with the same lady friend. Otherwise, the young man would type into the computer all day, in the same position; occasionally, he would touch his short hair with his long, white fingers. Or he would flex his muscles when suddenly turning around. Or raise his blue, lovely eyes right into the camera and by pure coincidence look straight at Officer Kampf - like an invitation, like a prayer, like an offering.

That Friday evening, Officer Kampf noticed that the young man was sad; he stayed late and his beautiful eyes were wrinkled with unpleasant thoughts. Officer Kampf looked with a shade of interest but also with disappointment: was this young man to be thrown into the swirl of life, was he to be sucked alive into the likes of passion and suffering? Was he to become yet another insignificant drama in the forgettable history of the insignificant people? Officer Kampf could have guessed that the lady friend – first name Anna, last name Ionescu, employee ID: 13350 -- is somehow involved; for all he knew, she seemed like trouble.

Whatever it was, Officer Kampf understood that it was of the utmost importance; he felt the young man's angst and pain and he even had an urge to help him, to tell him what he had learned about the world; to comfort him with chosen words, long, winding words he used to speak ages ago; to explain everything – from creation to murder, from dreams to realities; to rest his hand on the young man's shoulder, in a touch of human love and care.

The thought aroused him unexpectedly and violently. A primal, deep lightening ripped through his abdomen, with heavenly pain. His longtime abstinent body awoke with no mercy and in a short moment regained its rank and importance in his life. Officer Kampf reached to the screen, craving the young man's touch and closeness. Just as his fingers gently and eagerly followed the bodyline on the screen, the young man suddenly jumped off the chair and stuck his head close to the camera. "What's your name?" Officer Kampf read on the mute lips. "What's your name?"

In the miracle of being seen and felt through the impersonal camera, in the miracle of being addressed, of being acknowledged, Officer Kampf rose in a joyous, frustrated orgasm. It lingered in his flesh for seconds before sweetly disseminating through his whole body, in hot circles of divine glory. Incapable of thinking, Officer Kampf shut down the monitor in shame and love, to be dealt with later; inside his cube, Dante had fallen back into his chair, still not knowing the name of his cubicle neighbor.

CANTO II

Flowers shrug when I touch them. Trees bend in pain, in defense, when I reach for their fruit. I killed the entire grapevine in my grandparents' garden when I was five by picking up its sweet, black grapes. I am the anti-matter to the earth's flora; an unknown and therefore dangerous hybrid of human cells and inner Nature secrets, blended with ancient spells. I seem one of them and yet I do not grow and feel as they do.

I chose to live in sterile apartment buildings with a No Pets policy. I have a plastic plant in my living room and pictures of chickens in my kitchen. I've always liked animals but the fauna doesn't like me any better either. When I was four, I took up the difficult but rewarding task of taking care of six small orphan chickens at my grandparents' farm. They all died in separate, horrible accidents in less than a week. I suspect they have successfully managed to kill themselves out of my toxic love. They did not understand what I was and to them I must have been frightening as hell when I was petting them endlessly. It was probably as calming as it would be for a human being to be petted and loved by a dark, huge ghost they cannot relate to at any level.

Wise men spend years to become one with the Nature; I had to spend years to tear away from it. It was revealed to me the day I was born; the grass growing; the waves forming; the rain and the storm; I was one with them. I cried when the wind cried and I was hungry when the birds were. I screamed when giving birth and I died in struggles only to grow back, stronger. I was already dust before I had lived my first month on earth. There was no mask, no fairy tales, no beliefs in good and bad to protect me from Nature; I had to face it since the beginning.

My parents have conceived me in secrecy and fear, with the enlisted help of the village's witch – my aunt Profira. She was the best of us when it came to slipping under the radar of life; her house, a mud cottage with one room and an atrium, was built in the shadows of the hills between Romania and Ukraine. She had found a narrow numeric pattern there – a closed eyelid upon a lazy patch of grass. Silently, she had built her house and brought her things in over the months. She rarely spoke; she awoke at night, old and scared, and checked the numbers to make sure the eye hadn't opened to see her. That she still had one more day to live, one more hour, one more minute. That Death had not reached that place just yet.

For nine months, my parents lived there in silence. The risks involved were large; over generations, my family had grown to be a thorn in the paw of natural law. Nature was on to us; we had become an unknown life form and therefore prone to be eliminated. It was not as if Nature was a conscious entity who hated us; Nature simply was, and any foreign corpuscle was to be attacked and subdued – for the survival of the greater organism.

Nobody is supposed to fool the numbers; there is only one Master of the numbers and he is one with Earth and the Universe. One cannot go on cheating on life because it simply doesn't work for too long. One cannot have all the sweets and no bitterness; all light and no darkness; all love and no mistrust. Our ancestors simply have not negotiated the deal that way.

Having me was an act of defiance in a family that could hardly maintain its head count as it was. One more of us, especially one born into knowledge and truth, was an easy target. The danger was not that I was weak; the danger was that I could have been too strong. While my great-great-great-great uncle was an itch, I could have been a powerful cramp and therefore targeted for annihilation much faster. My parents though did what they had to do: produce an heir to give meaning to their lives and assure the continuity of the family through natural ways. They truly believed they could protect me and teach me all I needed to know. On the day of my birth, however, all hell broke loose.

It must have been the tension and anticipation in the house; my aunt cheerfully going about the business of preparing the holy water, the herbs and the spells for my arrival; my dad, knuckles white from pressure, holding my mom's hand. It must have been the humanity, the tenderness, the normality they all felt when such a common miracle was finally about to happen to them. Or maybe they just forgot to check the numbers that morning; maybe, when my mom started to feel the pain, old numbers shifted in a natural regression and new numbers took their place around the hills; maybe, as the birds started to squeak in the old tree, Nature had already felt another life about to enter its realm and hurried to receive it in its palm.

I came out in my usual fast and organized manner, head first, serious and self-conscious, preoccupied not to cause pain or embarrass anyone. My dad, with tears of joy on his cheeks, took me in his arms. "Profira!" he called, "it's a girl!" But there was no answer and when my dad turned around, he recognized the hideous face of his mistake written in bold new numbers around the window. My aunt was knocked out in the backyard, her heart stopped; the eyelid had opened with inquisitorial power; and in just a few moments, the biggest flood that the village has ever seen started from the suddenly anger waters of the Prut river.

"I gather you all got out all right", Lou commented.

"Yeah", I said. "My dad had a backup plan. He always does. There was another good path through the cornfield, and he carried my mom and me out. My aunt had died though – just before I was born."

"And so, my first memory is the gray water of Prut flowing into the house, up my dad's knees. Not a good greeting when you first arrive in the world." I continued.

"Not that I believe any of this… ", said Lou, "But you're still alive. If Nature was after you, how come you managed to live 33 years?"

"I found my ways." I said. "It's not that bad once you blend into the asphalt civilization; you're hard to track in the crowds. Besides, Nature has other problems except me and my pathetic life."

"So, in a way, you won?" asked Lou.

I laughed hard, sarcastically. You'd think that he would have known by now. You'd think that he saw all those medical books in my bedroom, stashes after stashes of female anatomy pictures and charts of symptoms and temperatures. You'd think he would have understand by now, after two years of living and breathing together, that Nature had won all the important battles so far, and that I had given up on my destiny a long time ago.

"Just hold me", I said, turning off the lights. He put his arms around me, warm, breezy, another misunderstood and loving ghost wandering the earth in disillusion and blind faith. Through the bedroom window, the moon looked upon me with pity.

* * *

Dante looked with emotion at his childhood home. Arlington was a much richer community nowadays, with all the dot-commers and AOL millionaires on a buying spree in Northern Virginia. His mom had kept the small house intact, almost as she purchased it 35 years ago from a Sears catalog.

Dante picked up the Saturday mail from the red rose-painted mailbox, smiling. His mother had a thing for roses. His childhood's plates and cups were painted with roses in different stages of beauty; the dining room and the kitchen had rose-print curtains, bows and tablecloths. It was all a pinky-reddish flower boom.

His mother was in the small garden behind the house, planting seeds around the white fence. She was chatting with the next-door neighbor. A squirrel looked at Dante from the big tall tree in the backyard, and then ran out of view.

"Hi, Lucia!" Dante yelled, carefully stepping around the sprinkle.

They called each other by their first name; it was a deal they made 30 years ago, one of the several secret deals that they forged out while trying to survive poverty and adversity and had nobody else but each other to hold.

"Dante!" his mother exclaimed. "Oh, my darling, what a surprise!"

"Hello, Mr. Saccas!" Dante said, waiving to the neighbor. "How are you today?"

"Oh, just fine, just fine", the neighbor answered; he was a skinny old man who looked just the same ever since Dante could remember. "Ah", he added, "You look *bellissimo*, what a pleasure to see you. Your mamma was just talking about you, what a good job you have. Bravo, bravo, it's a pleasure to see you."

"Just stopped by to see my mom, sir", Dante answered. "I just had a craving for those chocolate cookies she makes."

Lucia looked at him, smiling.

"Let's go inside, honey", she said, "I'll make you some tea."

An hour later, while Dante finished his sixth cup of tea, he finally got the courage to start the questions.

"Lucia", he said, "I need to talk to you about Dad."

She lost her smile; "Dad" was not a subject of conversation in her house, and her son knew it well.

"I know", Dante answered the silent accusation, "but something happened. I found Dad's name on a list of speakers for my Company."

"A list of what?" asked Lucia, suddenly cold and rational.

"Some speakers for some meeting", Dante said. "Why? Who would do that? Why would he be on a list? It is driving me crazy, mom. What do you make of this?"

"What meeting?" she asked again in the same tone of voice.

"The stupid shareholder meeting next Monday", Dante answered impatiently. "Does it matter?"

Lucia stood up slowly and went back to the kitchen. She washed the cups, then washed her hands carefully, again and again.

"Mom?" asked Dante, following her. "Does this mean he is alive? It has to mean at least that, right? Right?"

"I don't know", said Lucia. "I don't know more about you father than Mr. Saccas next door does. I swear this is the truth."

There was nothing he could hang on to. Not a small glimpse of hope, a clue. "You have to tell me about him, mom", he said, frustrated. "All you've ever told me was his name. I need to know what he was like, where he worked, what he liked, why he left."

Lucia sat down again, hands shaking. "It is very painful for me to talk about him, Dante", she said. "Don't you see how much pain that man has caused me? Why do you want to put me through this?"

Dante felt bad instantly; he had only thought about himself and had forgotten about her own feelings.

"I'm sorry", he said mildly, holding her hand. "I don't know why I came here to ask you about it. I mean, it's a Company memo, it's not like you can possibly know anything about it."

"That's right", she answered. "I don't know where he is or what has become of him, Dante. Maybe he is a speaker. Maybe he lives down the street. I don't know and I don't care to know. Do you understand me?"

He did not, but he pretended he did. He felt he had no right to bring back painful memories for her.

When he left, his mom waved him good bye from the front door and went back inside. Dante turned his head and, through the window, saw his mom on the phone. He smiled at her.

"You're leaving already?" asked Mr. Saccas, still cutting weeds in the garden.

"Yes, I have to go", answered Dante. "Nice weather today, huh?"

"Yes, indeed", said Mr. Saccas. "You come back soon, okay?"

"Sure thing", said Dante.

As he was getting into the car, Mr. Saccas hurried inside to answer the ringing phone.

--*

My first distinct memory, which I have never disclosed to Dante, was one of a truck out of control heading toward me. I was 3 years old and I was standing at the foot of the hill on Main Street, in my hometown. I was there shopping with my grandmother; while she was busy buying the bread, I saw the friendly man from the donuts shop waving at me. I waved back; he smiled at me and secretly made an inviting gesture – there were fresh donuts baking and I was offered the first bite.

I did not read the numbers; at that age, the smell of fried donuts was very tempting to me; besides, I had figured out my hometown by then and it was safe almost all over. A small, industrial city in the north of the Carpathians Mountains, it was an oasis of steel and asphalt that had kept Nature at bay. The numbers were flat and boring; there was nothing new being born or changed; there was a big 4 hanging in front of the Police station that has not moved an inch since I can remember.

In a happy enthusiasm, which I lost a long time ago, I sprang in the directions of the donuts; as I was crossing the street, I saw the truck. My grandmother screamed first, followed by the bread storeowner and then by the other people in the market. The donuts man did not scream; he looked at me and it was then that I saw the evil pattern clearly mirroring in his eyes.

The truck was out of control; later, people told me the brakes did not hold and the driver was terrified. But I have seen the driver's face – in those precious moments, all the numbers aligned and confessed to me; he was not scared. He was cold and determined, and he was no ordinary man; his lips were counting; his truck's trajectory seemed random but I have actually seen it carefully following an 8-star path which ended at the donuts shop's door. There was no mistake in my mind – I knew that I was the target.

I have played that scene in my mind many times. It awoke my extreme precision in navigating danger with nothing but instinct; to calculate trajectories and multiply ten-digit numbers in nanoseconds; always correctly, always consistently. It was that day when my whole power came out from inside my childish body and took over my life, never again to leave.

Because I just saw the solution with no effort; I saw the narrow gate I could escape through. As the truck wheezed past me, all I did was to move my foot one seventh of an inch and lose my equilibrium onto the 8-star pattern; it held me for a few moments, and it was all that I needed. My grandmother says that she saw me bending around the truck like a vine, tunneling it, filling out the gaps in the space that were available for my body to occupy without touching it.

But one more thing happened in that moment; I had been tested and I had now proven what I could do. I was a tumor on the normal, dying cycle of life; I was threatening the balance; I was to be destroyed. When the natural law acts, it is all-powerful; it has not only a second plan but a third plan and a fourth plan; it does not play mind-games and tricks; it is direct and true, as the keeper of life has to be. Nature saw that I was not easy to kill and saw that it might have to take its time to do so; but it also saw the opportunity to stop from repeating the same mistake it made when it let me be born into life.

As I regained my balance, one number changed slightly. I noticed it immediately and tried to move away from unstable, alive, unknown support. But I was not fast enough, and I felt it touching through my midriff as I was struggling to avoid it. It smoothly moved to form the forth pyramid, to take its place in the natural weight of things, leaving me crippled for life. My middle section never developed since; an eternal child inside, never to achieve maturity. I was isolated like a bad virus you cannot yet destroy, but you can contain.

I have never told this to my grandmother or anyone else in my family. They were so proud of me, of how I handled myself. They said I was very smart; but I wasn't. It was not a matter of being smart, but a matter of knowing things without having to think about them. To my family, I am their best creation yet; their absolute pride and joy; and being a woman, a natural advantage already, just makes me more precious in their eyes. To this day, 30 years later, I could not bring myself to tell them that in fact I was defeated long ago, while being tempted with a freshly baked donut.

I was having lunch with Dante that Sunday and he seemed distracted and sad. He was usually content with himself and self-absorbed in his own frame of mind; in the year since we've become "office buddies", I have never seen him so upset.

"What's up?" I asked him. "Your idiotic supervisor giving you grief?"

"Nah", he dismissed me with a gesture.

He had ordered the turkey hamburger with a side of broccoli instead of fries, which had the waitress wondering if Dante's gay.

Dante was way too good looking for a straight man. With his short haircut, high cheeks, steel-blue eyes, square chin, and a slim but obviously muscular body, you would have thought he is a model. He wasn't very smart either, which fooled people even more. I haven't seen one person to believe him when he was introduced as being a computer engineer. I suspect they all thought he was a movie actor trying to hide his secret life.

However, Dante had no clue whatsoever on the effect he had on people. A true programmer at heart, he preferred the darkness and isolation of his cubicle to any human interaction. He was happiest when left alone; and could not figure out why he never was. The only thing he did to groom himself was to keep his hair really short (an influence from his uncle, a former Jarhead), shower each morning, and wear clean clothes. He was a bit too obsessed with cleanliness.

Even then, when we were having lunch, I could feel the other females in the room looking at him.

"Hey, there's a cute chick smiling at you", I told him, pointing to an artificial looking blonde with a bit of a mustache. "The best of the suburbs comes to this place", I added, laughing.

"Whoa", reacted Dante, not even turning his head.

Sipping from his coffee, Dante suddenly looked straight at me with a sharp expression. "Do you know, Anna," he said, "what my first memory is?"

"My first memory", he continued, "is a truck out of control heading toward me. I was 3 years old and I was standing at the foot of a hill, up in Mount Airy. My mom had taken me to visit a friend in the countryside and we had stopped for a short break to admire the hills and the forest."

I looked back at him, sustaining his eyes. I did not see any danger; he was not channeling me or playing a game. His memory was genuine and the coincidence did nothing more than to reinforce that my belief that our destinies were somehow linked together.

"I remember the hills, the forest and the cows with big horns I had seen at a distance; ours was the only car we had encountered on the winding Clarksburg Road", he continued.

His mom was wearing a white dress with red cherries design and was extremely emotional that day. She had hugged him and kissed him all day, and whispered sweet words in his young ears. But then, as they drove up route 355 and further from the city, she had relaxed and started to enjoy the surroundings. When she stopped the car to take a better look at the beautiful landscape around them, she was happy and at ease; she whisked Dante out from the car, in a laughing circle; then they sat, hand in hand, and looked upon the green valleys.

The truck appeared out of nowhere, with a frightening noise, smoke coming out its huge cabin. It made a short stop at the top of the hill, like a furious monster looking for prey. They turned around to see it speeding downhill, out of control, covering both lanes of the road in sweeping destruction. It was headed towards them; in a second, his mom jumped in front of Dante in a desperate attempt to protect him.

Time seemed to freeze; from behind his mom, Dante could not see the monster but he could hear the abominable noise getting closer. He fixed his eyes on the red cherries prettily painted on his mom's dress; he thought of cherries and how they taste; he held to her dress, fearful, scared, reaching for her touch.

And then two strong arms took him and ran with him; in a confused, distorted vision, he followed the red cherries with his eyes; his mom was close. He screamed, loudly, but he could not hear himself; the truck passed somewhere above them, noise and all, and disappeared just as mysteriously as it had appeared, up the next hill and into the forest. Dante opened his eyes to find himself in the arms of Mr. Saccas, tucked under a small bridge; his mom was near them, shaking. She reached for him and held him tight, and he could finally embrace her and forget the monster.

"Oh, wow," I said, "that's quite a story. Where did Saccas came from?"

"It turns out he was going to the same friend we were going, and he saw the truck before we did", said Dante. "He had enough time to get out of his car and sweep us both under the bridge, fortunately. We were very lucky he happened to be there."

"So what else happened that day? I asked. Because I needed to know the whole story; I had a glimpse of a plot, a conspiracy or something like that, but I could not put my finger on it just yet.

"Nothing, really", said Dante. "We spent the day in Mount Airy at this friend of my mom's, a very nice lady. Then I fell asleep on the couch and when I woke up I was home in my bed."

I didn't want to say anything at that time. I ate my rice soup; I tried to cheer Dante up with office rumors about his supervisor being a transvestite; but in the back of my mind, I knew that someone was after him. That someone had planned to kill Dante that day, 30 years ago. That his mother and the convenient Saccas were somehow aware of it. If I knew something, it was survival – and I felt that Dante might need to learn a thing or two about it too.

"My name is Karen", the waitress burst suddenly in an emotional voice, while serving the peach-flavored ice tea.

By the end of that lunch, three people – the waitress, the blonde and a middle-aged man with a kid – had asked Dante out for coffee. He refused each of them. "See, Anna", he told me when we were finally outside, "that's why I don't go out much. You meet all sorts of freaks who want to talk to you and stuff."

--*

Dante came in Monday morning to find a voice mail message from his mother. "Dear", she had said, "I'm sorry I was so upset yesterday. Why don't you come by next weekend and we'll talk about more pleasant things? I'll put some chairs out on the porch. Please leave that memo alone; it won't do you any good to pursue that. Okay? Now take care. Bye." Dante shook his head; she could have called at home to apologize, instead of leaving him a message at the office. But he was not going to take her advice of dropping the memo investigation.

The secretary who wrote the speaker list memo lived in a cave on the dark side of Low Life Forms department. Her name was Victoria Queen and she was chewing gum when Dante shyly knocked at her door.

"What?" she barked.

"Hi", Dante said, putting on the left-cheek gap smile. "My name is Dante Portinari-Guelph."

"So?", the secretary asked. "You're from Sweaters? Tell them I'm not done yet. It's been a bitchin' week with all this freaking memos I gotta send. I'm doin' my best, okay? They don't have to send you here to punish me. I'm tryin', okay?" And she pointed out to her feet.

Dante realized that her feet were moving under the desk, knitting something that looked like a wool sweater.

"Oh, wow", he said, "you're quite talented. How did you learn to do that?"

The secretary looked at him carefully. She had heard the legend of a sweet talker who one day might come by and release her from her duties. It was a slim chance that this young man was going to save her – but he was definitely the first sweet talker she had seen since she had been hired at the Company.

"Well, honey", she said, "I'll tell you my story 'cause I like you and you should learn something from it. Like, read the fine print! Read the fine print!"

"Okay", said Dante, fascinated by the toes' dance under the desk.

"They hired me to send memos. I said: okay, sure, honey, no problemo. I can send some memos, sure. But then my second day on the job, my new boss comes in and installs this knitting station here. He says, he's like: you gotta knit me sweaters, hon. And I'm, like, whoa! You know, I used to work at Hecht's in Friendship Heights, okay? I mean, I don't do manual work, okay? He goes, yeah, okay, 'cause this is not manual. You gonna use your feet, so you don't breach the agreement and the contract we signed. I'm like, I don't remember anything of sweaters in my job duties, you know. And he laughs, and he's like: well, next time read the fine print!"

"Oh, geez…" Dante exclaimed sympathetically. "How many sweaters do you have to knit?"

"One a day, hon. One a day. If I don't finish the sweater I can't go home, you know. I'm behind, like, about 47 sweaters already and I've only worked here for two months. I haven't made it home in weeks."

"Oh, God", said Dante. "That can't be right. You know, my mom has a neighbor who used to be a lawyer. I'll ask him about this, because this doesn't seem right, you know. They have to let you go home, at least. That's just horrible."

"You do that, sweet talker", the secretary said. "Now, what are you looking for here?"

"So my name is Dante Portinari-Guelph", Dante said, emphasizing the words. "See, Portinari-Guelph with only *one* dash. Now, my father's last name is Portinari- - Guelph with *two* dashes and a space between the dashes. See? Because this is how everyone in his family was named, but I did not get the same right because everyone was pissed when he was never married to my mom in church, and they only had a civil ceremony. See? I have his last name but without being actually part of his family. Very subtle, right?"

"I have no idea what you're talking about", said the secretary. "I don't care about your name or your daddy's. Never heard of any of you in my life."

"Actually", said Dante, "you have. You sent a memo to shareholders, and my dad's name was in it. You see, he's been missing since I was like 1 year old and now you sent a memo with his name in it. See? I have to find him. You have to tell me why you put his name in that memo."

"Okaaay", said the secretary. "You're a cute boy and all, and I feel sorry you lost your daddy, but I know nothing about it. I don't write the memos, I only send them. They come to me from some other secretaries in other departments. I just send them to where they tell me, okay?"

"Well, why did you send me a memo addressed to shareholders then?" asked Dante. "I am no shareholder. You see, you must have made a mistake. Sent the wrong memo to the wrong people, maybe with the wrong names in it. I mean, if it's a mistake of any kind, I want to know before I get my hopes up here."

The secretary looked through the papers on the desk, shaking her head. "Is it this one?" she asked, holding a piece of black paper with white letters on it.

"Yes", said Dante. "that's the one. See? You put me on the list of shareholders – there is my name, with *one* dash. And see, that's my dad's name right there. With *two* dashes."

The secretary rolled her eyes. "Look, honey", she said, losing the accent and the funny talking. "I may not be fast at knitting sweaters, and I may be stupid enough to let a bald man give me a bad job – but I am not a bad secretary. I made mistakes, of course, but I'm a good person, you know. I know my job. I'm organized, I have my own system that I invented, you see?"

She pulled out a drawer with files, aligned in straight rows. "I don't trust computers *that* much", she continued. "I have my own filings here, and they're always better than the damn machines. Okay? So let's see here: Shareholders Names and Addresses. Here you are, boy: Dante Portinari-Guelph, 52 Amber Road, Suite 205, Gaithersburg, Maryland 20878. Number of private shares: 500,000. Shares granted on: June 3rd, 1969. See? I made no mistake, hon. You *are* a shareholder."

"500,000 shares?" Dante laughed. He would have laughed even louder, but his address was correct and the date mentioned in there was his birthday. "I don't have 500,000 shares of anything", he said. "Where did you get that number? What are you trying to do here?"

"Take it easy, sweet talker", the secretary answered. "I made this list two months ago, when I started to work here. There was still the old management, on my first day at work. I went on to training, had a free lunch, was introduced to people, and made my own files with addresses. I sent a beautiful memo that day. Mr. S., the boss who hired me, was such an angel. But then, the next day hell broke loose. New management, new job, and I had to start knitting. Poor Mr. S., I don't even know what became of him. He might be knitting sweaters somewhere too, poor man."

She sighed deeply. "Look," she told Dante, who was sitting in silence trying to make sense of the information, "why don't you go ask the Shareholders board. I mean, if it's a mistake, they should be able to fix it. There's nothing much I can do from here. All I know is that they sent me the memo and they told me to send it to all shareholders in the Lower Earth. Okay?"

"Okay", said Dante. "There is a Shareholders board?"

"Sure thing, hon. Here, let me write you down their office number. They're right upstairs in the Medieval department."

"Okay, then. Thanks for you help and I'll come visit again sometime."

"Hon?" the secretary called after him.

"Can you bring me a cup of coffee? I'm stuck here to the damn knitting station."

"Wouldn't you rather have a bottle of orange juice?" asked Dante. "I don't think coffee is such a good idea. You know, it's bad for you. My mom just told me about this article about how coffee can cause cancer and make you infertile. It's really scary."

"Fine, I'll take orange then", she decided. "Good luck with your daddy, kid. And don't forget: Always read the fine print!"

--*

Officer Kampf had watched Dante's wanderings with great interest. He had completely given up his standing pose at the glass gates, and pulled himself a chair from the conference room right in front of the monitors. He had never before watched the monitoring system closely; he was not sure he was supposed to. His job was to sit at the gates, for what he understood in the short briefing he had received when starting his job. But there was someone in need of help out there; a young man, whose name he just found out after listening in the discussion with the secretary, was searching for his missing father, alone and clueless in the cruel, complicated jungle of the Company.

Officer Kampf thought about it for a while. He did not like to rush into anything. There was a possibility that the young man was simply wrong, or lying; there was even a possibility that Officer Kampf's boss had hired him as bait, to get Officer Kampf fired. But his instinct denied these theories; one look at Dante and it was clear to everyone that this was an honest, beautiful person.

He watched Dante taking the elevator to the Medieval floor and getting off with a confused look on his face. It was pretty clear Dante had never visited that floor before; he stood in the front of the secured glass doors and waved his badge in front of the electronic reader. Nothing. Dante tried again, unsuccessfully.

Officer Kampf smiled – obviously, Dante did not have enough security clearance to visit that floor. His badge access was most probably only for the Lower departments, floors 3 and down. The Medieval was the 5th. Officer Kampf did not hesitate much this time – there was finally an opportunity to help and he took it right away.

Dante, who had figured out his lack of access too, was about to turn around and get back in the elevator, when an electronic beep stopped him. The security light was green and, in front of him, the glass door opened slowly. "Wow", he said loudly, "so at this floor it takes a couple of minutes until your badge opens the door. Ha!"

Officer Kampf laughed heartily. With fast moves, he switched the images on the monitors trying to follow Dante's path through the cubicle rows. He was heading to the department manager's office, hidden in the Rainbow at the end of the Castle. A minstrel sang sadly in the lunchroom while receiving a fax. Officer Kampf enabled the sound option and waited for Dante to knock at the manager's door.

And then, an alarm sounded. Officer Kampf jumped off the chair and immediately took his position at the door; he stood there for a few minutes, waiting for something terrible to happen. The worst scenarios went through his mind – maybe they saw him using the monitors, leaving his post, falling in love, spying. Maybe they were coming up to fire him and shame him.

But nothing else happened. The alarm, which, he now realized, had sounded too muffled to be close to him, stopped for good. He heard an ambulance downstairs and peeked out of the window to see a couple of people being taking away by paramedics. He stepped backwards, looking at the monitors only to discover the same old picture everywhere.

Officer Kampf breathed deeply. Taking his seat again, he listened in different rooms until he got the whole story. It turned out that all the fuss was about some bad coffee in the lunchroom at the 2nd floor. It made a few people sick and they called the ambulance. On the right screen, Officer Kampf saw the knitting secretary getting up and dismantling the knitting station with a solid boot kick. She was jumping around in happy circles. As it soon made it to Officer Kampf's ears, it turned out that her boss had drunk the bad coffee and was sick. Not only that, but when he got sick he had spilled coffee on his desk, completely destroying the small print on her contract.

Officer Kampf shook his head. A theory was forming in his mind; although he already knew that Dante was no ordinary man, he had never realized the terrific magnitude of his reach. There was forgiveness then for his own abject sins – because Dante was love in its purest form, and no one could resist it. He should have seen it – a simple, clean mind, an abstinent body, those caring eyes – Dante was a savior with a miraculous touch.

Officer Kampf bowed in the direction of everything, feeling relief and tenderness. He gave thanks for things he could not name. He converted to a new religion, right there. All that it took was a pot of bad coffee in the lunchroom on the 2nd floor.

--*

I was running out of time and I knew it. I could feel it in every fiber of my tired body, and in the strong, invisible cords linking me to my family. Even though I had moved from Romania to the US, our bond was not diminished by space; it simply did not have space as a dimension of its existence.

I had avoided talking with my parents for the last two months. I wrote short, cold email messages telling them how busy I was at work with the Company going public and all that. It's not like I could ever lie to them –

because they know me so well. But we like to keep appearances in my family. We don't make scenes and say great words, and throw our hearts on the table. We'd rather write cold, short messages rather than say it straight as it was. But they knew things were wrong.

They have tried to find me a mate since I was 16. It was very important that I have children, hopefully lots of them. I was the last one in the family who could carry on life, the best suited because of my instinct, my femininity, my beauty. Attracting unsuspecting males was easy; converting them to our beliefs – very possible. The probability rate on that was almost 95%. Nobody in my family understood my complete denial of any relationships they suggested; my absolute frigidity; my terror when they would even mention mating.

My parents tried to protect me; they said I was still too young, they said I was too special; too smart; too gifted; all the good things they could think of. That the man for me was not born yet. And through it all, I could not bring myself to tell them the truth; to destroy their hopes with a few words.

"I think that you should tell them", Lou commented. We were watching the season finale of Friends and all that talk about babies had made me sad.

"I mean", he continued, "they probably know that there is something wrong anyway, right? You'll feel better if you get this off your chest."

"I need just a little more time", I said. "I know what I'm doing. I just have to find the 2-2-9. I think it still exists somewhere around here."

Lou looked at me surprised. "What are you talking about?" he asked. "How exactly is the 2-2-9 going to reverse 30 years of underdevelopment?"

"2-2-9 is the big one", I told Lou. "It's the ancient spell, the little magic left over in the world by the old gods. It's fixing and repairing all that needs to be fixed and repaired. It's the magic number, Lou. And I know it's around here somewhere."

"Like, in Gaithersburg?" he asked. "There's nothing in Gaithersburg. Only houses and boredom, and a train."

"There are still farms", I said. "There are still plants, parks and forests. I think it might still be here. I feel it sometimes, breathing easily, close."

Lou went to the kitchen, still shaking his head. "Want some tea?" he asked.

"Okay", I said.

It had taken me a long time to locate Gaithersburg, MD as the possible place where a little magic still lives, dormant. It was like a joke of the old gods; they had left all their spells across Europe, many in Africa, lots in South America, but they had never made it to the north of the continent. People here were rational and hard working but knew no spells. And yet, all the signs eventually pointed to Gaithersburg.

"You see", I told Lou, "if I just find the 2-2-9, then I will be normal. I can finally take on my duty and give some meaning to my life. I can fulfill my destiny. I can fight instead of laying low. I will have all the aces, you see?"

"Well", he agreed, "fine. So, have you looked for it?"

"Every day", I said. "It's just not working, for some reason. I looked everywhere and I see no clear patterns, no equations. It's like a primordial mess here. Plants, trees and insects are mixing their lives together. I can't single anything out."

Lou brought in the tea in my favorite golden cup. "Don't worry, you'll find it", he said. We both smiled. "I know you will. If I can help, let me know", he added. I could always count on him for the right words; for the supportive words; for keeping me almost sane.

He was once young and blond; childish, pretty and fragile; a sick young man remembered by someone in another time. A lung disease had left blue, delicate marks throughout his face, his hands.

"You are so young", I said tenderly. "When did you die?"

"I don't know anymore", he turned suddenly and left for the kitchen. "It was a long time ago."

I lingered a bit more on the image surfacing from my memories; it was comforting, somehow, to finally put a face to my resident ghost.

I had bought the condo on the first visit, mostly because of Lou; I had seen him there in the kitchen, making tea out of old leaves that only I could smell. He was sad; tall, a shadow; a graceful presence that touched me. When the real estate agent left the room, I talked to him; he had his burdens, his prejudices, his wrong ways; but overall he was genuinely friendly and happy with interesting company – which I could definitely offer.

He had been taking care of me; baking cookies and boiling tea every night; keeping me company at the window when I was spying Nature's territory outside; being the voice of reason in my hectic life. He was comforting; he had no desires, no unfinished business; no wish to leave my kitchen. He liked daily rituals and familiar places, and even though he was willing to listen to my stories he never believed me completely.

And he was always right too. That evening, I gathered a little more strength and I thought of new strategies for my search. I would wait for the fog before the dawn before driving into the park; I would cast a few Romanian spells for good-luck and for rain; I would ask people about unknown places around Gaithersburg. That night, I fell asleep full of new hope.

The next morning, both my grandfathers died.

CANTO III

If you can read this, I must have died too. I must have melted my story back into the very matter that we are all made of, and resurfaced gently in your genes, like a warning, like a lesson. You might just be remembering me.

I have a memory of the flesh; I live openly in the anamnesis. For short, painfully delighting moments, past becomes present and present fades into past. My body remembers; in slow movements, selective images and sensations from the forgotten collective unconsciousness come back ghost-like into my blind flesh and, through it, surface back into brief existence. The vanilla taste of a battle somebody's won; the honey-like sweetness of another's touch; and sometimes, late at night, the spicy, multi-colored, ecstatic force of lust.

The memories belong to me as much as they belong to those who have lived them; I am nothing but a mirror, an open gate to them. I am the keeper of the thread that cuts through all of us, linking us, remembering us; reminiscence is what makes us grow stronger and wiser with each generation. I may myself be only a memory of the flesh, brought back to life by someone's reverie; someone or something might have remembered my life for a brief moment; and any moment now, I might just have to go back into their dream.

As my grandfathers died, their memories transpired immediately through my palms, sweating out small strings of equations and knowledge. They were living in me because they were now part of the collective memory.

My grandfathers' sudden death, at the same second, in different locations and circumstances, was a heavy blow. Our family was losing ground fast, and I knew that it was mostly my fault; since I was crippled, I had refused to contribute to the family's needs; I had left them an ocean behind, alone, older by each day, weaker by each day. They have given me so much and I could not give them anything in return. Nobody in my family was blaming me for their deaths; there were no accusations, even though, had I chosen another path of numbers, we could have all been alive for longer. And I would have had in a second if I could, and they all understood that.

Still, when my grandmother called me that morning, my voice was ridden with guilt and remorse. There was no need to put it into words; there was no need for a telephone either, but pain travels easier through technology in our family.

"Are you okay?" I asked.

"We are okay", she answered, voice muffled. There was only one telephone in their village and she had had to walk two miles to get to it.

I couldn't think of anything else to say; we stood there in silence, I, in a condo in a suburb of Washington DC, she, in an old phone booth in the north of Romania. Thoughts exchanged fast; there was danger; there were mysterious blackouts and accidents; stars would appear overnight, new numbers would be born and changed every day. It was like Nature had put some resources into decoding our algorithms; trying out our defenses, hacking into our carefully constructed protection.

"It is unsafe for you there", I told her. "Come move with me here in America. We can all live here for a while. There are few hidden dangers here; people are tough and blind to the numbers. We'd be safe for some time."

"You know I can't", she answered. "We are nothing without our roots. You are different, you are stronger. You can live far away from here and still feed from these lands; but we can't. We've built our patterns on these particular hills, our maps trace through these particular rivers. If we step away from here, we'd be unprotected."

"I can come get you", I offered. "I'll take you through everything, I'll hide you behind my own shadow. I can do it, I know I can."

"It's okay", she said. "You better protect yourself and use your knowledge to survive and breed. We are becoming obsolete. You are the only one who has to survive for us to win."

"I called you for something else", she said after a pause. "Do you remember what I taught you when you were little? Our secret?"

"Of course I remember", I said. "It's one of my precious memories, you should know that."

"I am not sure I can read you anymore", she confessed. "Sometimes you are a stranger to me. It must be because I am so tired nowadays."

"I think you can still read me", I said. "I'm in you as much as you are in me. Nothing will change that."

"My memory is failing me sometimes now", she said. "That's why I wanted to be sure you remember our talks. You have to remember."

"Don't worry", I said. "I have no choice but to remember. I'll remember for the both of us."

"Good", she said. "Because I think that I might have hit on something there, something we never relied on or took in our formulas before. I think I saw that as something that might help you. I don't know what demons you are fighting, but I know they are strong and they keep you from your duty. Our talks – what we talked about – might be of help to you. Promise me you'll explore that path."

"But there are no numbers there", I said. "I have no power there, you know it."

"I don't think it matters", she said. "There is a chance you may find what you're looking for, a slight chance, but one I can offer you before it's too late. You know that is never very clear, but there is definitely a probability for success."

"Okay", I said. "I'll think about it. I'll run some of my checks, okay? I promise."

But I had no intention of doing so. The subject of her religious outbursts was not interesting to me; I have heard that, as they get older, people tend to grow in their faith; for me, that subject was silly. When you have to fight for survival every day, you stop believing in angels.

I saw her through the eyes of my grandfather, as he remembered her. Young, beautiful; with wild green eyes, dark hair; a princess of royal blood living in poverty and silence in a forgotten village in the hills; carrying secrets and heavy facts on her small shoulders; deeply mysterious, dangerous, fluid like water; irresistible to him.

There was love of the divine type; there was love by not loving, by being beyond their beings; a touch was precious; it meant so much and it was so powerful, the numbers would cascade around them in sparks of light. Their embrace dressed up their bed in gold.

For the first time in my life, I was getting first-hand knowledge of my close family. My grandfathers were talking to me and filing their memories in a hurry, at once, overwhelming me with fresh, tasty information. They were breaking the silence. I laughed, harshly, guiltily. It felt good.

--*

Dante knocked at the Medieval castle's door with a blank mind; although he was pretty certain this was all a mistake, there was also this uncomfortable – the feeling that something might escape him, that he had not counted all possibilities.

"Are you Valois' assistant?" the manager asked as soon as Dante stepped in.

He was sitting alone at a long, wooden table. At his right, a large, dark wizard was combing his white beard.

"That's my lawyer, son", the manager said, following Dante's eyes. "So, where's the stuff Valois sent?"

"I'm sorry", answered Dante, "I think I am not the person you're expecting."

"Don't you leverage your position, boy", the manager yelled. "I've developed business processes since before you were born."

"Sir," Dante tried again, "my name is Dante Portinari-Guelph, with *one* dash. I don't know who Mr. Valois is. I am here to ask you about my mistakenly being recorded as a shareholder."

"Huh?" the manager screamed. "We make no mistakes here in the Medieval, son. If I say you're a shareholder, then you're a damn shareholder. There, let me see."

He pulled out a Palm Pilot from somewhere underneath his black cloth and rapidly moved the stylus up and down.

"What's your name again? Da Vinci?" he asked.

"Dante Portinari-Guelph", Dante answered patiently. "With *one* dash."

"Yeah", the manager said after moving the stylus a few more times, "you're a shareholder all right. You're on my list. 500,000 shares, exactly. Awarded on June 3rd, 1969."

"Sir", Dante sighed, "there's gotta be a mistake. I have no shares whatsoever. All my investments are in the 401(k) plan at the Company and they just lost all value with the market going down and all. How can I be on your list when I don't own any shares?"

"Wait a minute", he manager said. "There's some flag set out here in the database. Wait a minute, let me cross-reference it."

Dante waited patiently, curiously peeking at the big wizard. The wizard peeked back.

"Son", the manager said, and his voice had trembled a bit, "you're right and I'm wrong and this is all a mistake. You don't own any shares. See, this flag in the database was changed as if you were a shareholder; but you're not."

"That's what I thought", Dante said, relieved. Now that that was settled, there was a nice possibility that the Low Life secretary had sent a completely wrong memo.

"However", the manager continued, "there's a guy in here called Christian Portinari-Guelph who *is* a shareholder. 30 million shares, awarded November 1st, 1968."

"Is that last name with *two* dashes?" Dante wanted to know.

"Yep", the manager answered. "Wait a minute, wait a minute", he continued. "Ah, the damn flag is set for him too. Sorry, son, he's not a shareholder either. What the hell has happened to my beautiful database?!"

Turning his head back in fury, the manager yelled: "Where's the jester?"

"Wait just a wee bit more", he told Dante. "I'm gonna straighten this out in a jiffy. See, I'm new here and we've just implemented this database change last week."

"Oh, okay", Dante approved, understandingly.

Two security guards bolted through the door carrying a tired, dirty jester between them.

"What did you sabotage this time?" the manager yelled at him. "Did you switch flags in the database just to confuse all these people and make me look bad? Didn't you have enough time in the Tower to regret all that you've snitched to the HR department?"

"I did all and I did nothing", the jester answered. Underneath his colorful dress, Dante could see remains of a cheap business suit. The jester's hat had felt backwards, giving him the appearance of a crazed drunkard.

"I was in your computer and I am still there. You are bad boss. You are bad boss."

"Take him back!" the manager yelled. "Yo, Oz," he turned to the wizard, "maybe you can teach him some business etiquette, damn jester."

"I cannot sing anymore!" screamed the jester as he was dragged out. "I was hired to sing and to dance while giving my stock report in the morning! I loved dancing for the king!"

The wizard bowed and followed the jester out of the room, with a last long look at Dante's muscular arms.

"I don't think you can treat your employees like that", Dante said indignantly.

The manager shrugged, looking again into his Palm Pilot.

"This jester has sabotaged me ever since I took this position", he said. "First, he gives me stock tips in rhymes. I mean, that's not what I expect from my employees. Then, he criticizes every move I make, and praises the old manager. Next thing I know, he's sneaking into the mainframe room and changes bits here and there, just enough to cause trouble to honest young men like yourself."

Dante could not find anything else to say.

"Now, it's all taken care of", the manager said triumphantly, closing the cover of his PDA with a click. "The mistake is corrected; none of you Portinari *dash* da Vinci folks owns any stock in the Company. Okay?"

"Okay", said Dante. "I have one more question. How can anyone have shares awarded in 1968?" he wanted to know. "At that time, the Company probably didn't even exist. I think I've learned that in was created in January 1969."

"Hmm...", the manager wondered. "I couldn't tell you, son. I told you I'm new here. You can inquire, I guess, at the Department of History and Archives. They ought to know."

"Okay", said Dante, preparing to leave. "Thank you for correcting that error."

"No problem, son. Say, if you go to the History department, could you do me a favor and give Valois this letter?"

Dante took the folded document from the manager's hand. On its back, his fingers felt the warmth of the red wax seal.

"I sure can, sir. Thanks again."

Dante closed the gate after him. Near the elevators, the wizard was waiting for him.

"Hi", he said.

"Hi", answered Dante. "You know, I hope that jester will be okay."

"We are all nothing but slaves of our contracts", the wizard shrugged. "I am not happy either since the new management changed my job description into Black Magic instead of White Magic. I used to help people; now I just punish them. People used to like me and invite me to their parties and Happy Hours. Now, all I get is a reduced salary and loneliness."

"Can they do that?" Dante asked. "Can they just change what you do and you have to take it?"

"It's in the contract", the wizard said. He opened his arms with a majestic gesture of impotence. "It was written and we can only follow."

"Have you read the fine print?" Dante asked. "I was just talking with someone today about the importance of fine print. Have you checked it out?"

The wizard looked puzzled. "Why, I didn't even know there was some fine print in our contracts."

"Of course there is", Dante said helpfully. "There always is."

"I'll look", the wizard said. "Where are you heading?"

"The History department", Dante answered. Do you happen to know what floor that's on?"

"It's right upstairs, 7th floor", answered the wizard. "So, would you like to have lunch sometime?"

"Oh, thanks", Dante said in a hurry. "I can't stand lunch."

And with that, he stepped into the elevator that Officer Kampf had dutifully brought up for him.

It was already 4:00 PM and all departments were closing at 5:00. But Dante felt full of energy and ready to take the next step. He decisively pushed the 7th floor button in the elevator.

At the Medieval floor, the wizard dug out his contract from his dark office and read the fine print; it was clearly stated that he should not perform any Black Magic. With a cry of joy, he passed the Dragon and ran to the Tower to free the jester. By that evening, he was at a party having beer with his grateful colleagues, telling tales of a man who came to free up all sufferers.

--*

I woke up with burning eyes, out of breath. I had fallen asleep watching TV; Lou was nowhere to be seen. I coughed harshly, trying to clear my throat of a dry, fearful sensation. The images then came back to me straight and at once, violent and raw, just as they had been born out of my chaos of memories only a few minutes ago. I had been dreaming of myself as a baby – but I was my paternal grandfather, looking at me from a different body and another mind; the memory must have been deeply buried inside him, to dissolve into my consciousness only this late and unexpectedly.

I replayed the scenes one by one, slowly. I was 2 months old, asleep in an old wooden crib. I was also standing near the crib, an older man, smiling; I was looking at myself with love, a feeling I had never known before. Painfully aware of both sides, I let the feelings come up in plain view, slowly, clearly. That love felt good; I was able to grasp it through my sleep, with that instinctive accuracy children have. I also recognized the chimney in my grandparent's 2-room house, the familiar smell of bread and milk of their kitchen; the minuscule, fine numbers floating around my crib like a light-blue spider web – a spell my grandparents had woven for me as a child.

Suddenly, I slipped into a trap. I held my breath a fraction of a second longer, caught in a colored dream; it felt so soft and relaxing; out of curiosity, I held my breath again, following the beautiful rainbow deeper and deeper into unconsciousness. By the time my grandfather noticed that something was wrong, I was clinically dead.

My grandfather let out a horrified scream; my grandmother and my aunt Virginia ran inside. I was not moving; I was cold and my face was blue; the numbers stumbled, starting to change into a rigid diagnostic. My aunt Virginia whisked me out of the crib onto another room; my grandfather helped her by opening the doors and frenetically searching through the dresser's drawers. My aunt violently pushed everyone out of the room; when I woke up in her arms, there was a strong smell of lavender in the air; she was crying loudly, holding me tight. She had brought me back.

I caught my breath, shocked by this unexpected fact that materialized right into my quiet evening. I had never known that I was once dead for 35 minutes; nobody ever mentioned this amazing information to me. That could explain some traits that were not inherited and that seemed like gifts made in error by some ironic force – like my ability to keenly remember the lives of all dead people. It could also explain the fury, the anger, the disbelief I was receiving from any form of life primitive enough to remember what really matters.

"Lou!" I called weakly. "Lou, are you here?"

He came, worried; he brought me the blanket, the red pillow; he took my hand and tapped it softly, lovingly. "What happened?" he asked, "What happened?"

"I just remembered that I died", I cried. "My aunt Virginia used some kind of spells to bring me back, but I was truly dead for a little while. I had gone deep down, so deep I couldn't find my way back."

"That's okay," Lou smiled. "Many people die for a few seconds and they are brought back. You know, you've seen those movies when the doctors start to electrocute them with those devices, and then the heart starts beeping again on the monitor. It's not big deal, honey. It happens all the time."

"But my aunt didn't use any of those devices, she used magic," I sobbed.

"So, what's the difference?" Lou asked. "Do you think science is purer or cleaner than magic? Why shouldn't you use either if you can?"

"It was wrong," I said. "I can feel it so clearly, it was wrong. My grandfather thinks it was wrong, too. I don't know what she did, what if she did something horrible to revive me? She had to pay a price to someone or something, what price did she pay for my life? Did she sell my soul? Why the smell of lavender? I don't know any uses for lavender except for a love potion. I am freaked out. I am *freaked out*."

"Why don't you just ask her?" Lou said. "Talk to her, you'll feel better."

My aunt Virginia did not have a phone. She lived alone in a small house in the far north of Romania. I knew all about her house; I used to play there when I was a child; I knew where she kept her herbs, her snake; where the country wine sat in the cold basement, outside in the backyard; where her hens came to sleep at night.

"I would have to send a letter," I told Lou. "If I'm lucky, it will actually get there and not be stolen by the Romanian postal workers."

That night, as my aunt Virginia went to bring up the pickled cabbage for dinner, the number that locked her basement door squared spontaneously. She couldn't get out; her weak screams were lost in the falling snow. By morning, she had come to me in my memories.

--*

With the quiet help of Officer Kampf, Dante stepped right through the glass doors guarding the History department. It was deserted. Piles after piles of papers, papyruses, parchments, 8-inch floppy disks and CD ROMs were the only décor of the 7th floor. Dante carefully wandered around, following the signs on the wall pointing out the Department Head's office.

"Mr. Valois?" he asked carefully, peeking through the door into the dimly-lit room.

"Come in!" came the answer from inside, and Dante entered with confidence.

It was dark and very hot. Dante blinked a few times, trying to get used to the lack of light.

"Mr. Valois?" he asked again.

A tall, big man moved towards him with unexpected easiness. Very close to Dante, he studied him with green, sharp eyes.

"Who the hell are you?" asked Valois. His voice thundered over Dante's head, moving the air around in frightened waves.

"My name is Dante Portinari-Guelph", said Dante. "With one dash", he added by force of inertia and immediately regretted it. Valois seemed to react very badly at the mention of the dash, for some reason. His eyes minimized into green lines and his forehead drew heavy wrinkles.

"Dante?" Valois repeated in an angry but cautious voice. "Portinari? Guelph?"

"Yes, sir", Dante confirmed and stopped short of bringing up the dash again.

"What do you want?" Valois asked. "There is nothing here of interest. People lived, people died, never learned, and they left too little behind. That's all there is to History. Absolutely useless. We're liquidating this whole department."

"Well, sir", Dante began philosophically, "I wouldn't say that. History carries important answers and clues to the future…"

"Bullshit", Valois laughed. "So what do you want?"

"Actually, there's been a mistake with me and my dad showing up in this database of shareholders of the Company, even though I don't even know how a stock certificate looks like and my dad has been, like, missing for 30 years…"

"So why should I care?" Valois interrupted with a gesture of impatience.

"Well, we fixed that shareholder mistake, but then there was a detail in there about some stock being released in 1968, and I started to wonder how that can be, when the Company wasn't even publicly traded at that time. So I figured you guys here in History might know all about it and set it straight for me."

Valois hesitated a tiny moment. He measured Dante with his eyes, up and down, left to right. He smiled, then he changed his mind and he grinned. Then he thought for a while and decided to smile again.

"Sit down", he told Dante, shoving him gently to a black leather chair.

"Okay", said Dante, "but I can't stay too long because I have some reports to fill out…"

"You seem such a smart guy", Valois took a friendly tone, "I'm sure you can write reports in a jiffy, huh?"

Dante sat down in the comfortable chair, smiling.

"Actually", he said, flattered, "I've developed a program that would write most of them for me…"

As he was talking, the chair moved suddenly underneath him and a strong metal band sprang across his chest, holding him prisoner.

"Hey…" he tried to protest. Valois kicked the chair onto the wall forcefully, hurting Dante's knees.

"Hey!" Dante screamed. "What the…?"

"What are you doing here, boy?" Valois asked again. "Who sent you? And this time, no more playing stupid."

Before Dante could think of something, he saw Valois pushing a button on his desk. A drawer with unusual utensils popped open right under Dante's frightened nose.

"But I am stupid!" Dante confessed in horror, watching Valois maneuvering a large metal tongue. "I don't know anything!"

"I thought you were dead", Valois said with hatred. "They told me you were dead, you and your precious daddy. I thought we got rid of his seed forever."

"Sir", Dante tried, "you must be mistaking me for someone else..."

"Shut up!" Valois thundered again. "You're gonna answer everything I ask you, you understand? Because today I will do a good deed for the human race and kill you, as I should have done thirty years ago. If you want to die fast, you better tell me everything you know. Or else you will suffer all the pain I am able to inflict upon your worthless body. I have to tell you I was schooled in the Inquisition ways."

Dante's mind went blank, in shock. He was in the hands of a mad murderer and he didn't know how to handle it. For moments, all he heard was the eerie silence of the empty 7th floor; he felt the heat in the room forcing sweat out of his whole body.

"Is there a problem here, Mr. Valois?" a loud, cheerful voice broke the tension. They both turned around to see the imposing stature of Officer Kampf in the doorway.

"No problem", said Valois dismissively, "go away".

"I have to take the boy with me, sir", Officer Kampf announced softly. "He is wanted upstairs on the 30th."

Valois hesitated; Officer Kampf delicately touched his gun, still smiling. "I have to take the boy upstairs", he repeated. "We don't want to upset the people upstairs, now, do we, Mr. Valois?"

With an angry gesture, Valois clicked away Dante's strands. "Fine", he said. "I'll talk to them later."

Officer Kampf helped Dante out of the chair with a tender arm. "I appreciate your cooperation, sir", he told Valois as he was taking Dante out of the door.

"Make sure they know I cooperated", Valois said.

Outside the chamber of horror, Dante breathed deeply, leaning on the strong arm of Officer Kampf. "Thanks", he mumbled. In his pocket, crumpled, forgotten, was the letter addressed to Valois he was supposed to deliver.

CANTO IV

"You wouldn't *believe* what happened to me today," Dante said excitedly. "I was almost tortured and killed by a guy in the History department."

"A Marketing guy?" I asked calmly. Dante's imagination was the size of a 4-year old's who sees unicorns at his window; he mixed reality and fantasy with the innocence of a child, as if, in his own way, he could also see more than the cold and boring cubicles of a cold and boring corporation. He had his own names for departments and teams, and he moved in a parallel universe of his own as he was making his way through the building.

"I don't know," Dante answered. "Some kind of boss of some sort, I don't know. He had an office so he must be the boss of somebody. "

We were having a beer at Wings & Claws, a Gaithersburg neighborhood bar hidden between respectable, family-oriented stores in the mall. On the counter, a cockroach stepped defiantly towards us; it stopped and ran back all of the sudden; it must have felt my presence.

"I didn't even say anything to him," Dante continued. "I was just there to deliver this letter and ask a simple question – how come the company gave away stock in 1968 if they became publicly traded in 1969. I know it's a stupid, unimportant question but I was on a high from talking with all these other people. I started to enjoy talking. It wasn't *that* bad."

I first met Dante at a Company Happy Hour a year ago, and I felt nothing when our eyes met. There was no resistance in him; he simply existed. If not packaged in such an attractive bundle, he would have been transparent to all things. He was cornered by a bunch of people who wanted to talk with him; some would hand him business cards, which he would promptly discard into an ashtray on the bar. He seemed uncomfortable with all the attention he was getting; he smoothly made his way out of the crowd and into my direction.

Looking back, I should have seen a pattern there; how our trajectories through the room spiraled into a game, a tease; how we both ended up talking and joking. I should have recognized that we were very much alike, or at least that each of us had some qualities of some value to the other. It seemed a coincidence at the time, but I should have known better – I knew that there are no coincidences.

"So what happened?" I asked. "Did you just go in there and the guy attacked you?"

Dante related the full story of his incredible day, gesticulating frantically with the beer bottle. "That man was *crazy*, I'm telling you," he ended.

"I think you just bumped into an evil one," I said. "There are some people like this, simply evil."

I should know; I've met a few myself. When I was 4, my mom stepped on an old woman's foot when we were shopping in the crowded farmer's market. As it turned out, the woman had a painful blister and she was a nasty witch who then spent the next year stalking and terrorizing my mother. I remember finding freaky omens outside our door; the water in a pot turning bright red when boiled; dead birds being thrown through our window; spells floating in the air, combing the numbers into black integrals.

I did not understand what happened at first; her magic was dislocating some patterns but it was basically harmless to us; we could easily defend our house and ourselves. I did not understand why she started, why she persisted; I could see that her foot had healed, yet she had not given up her revenge. My mom explained to me about evil, how it just surfaces in some people and takes control, and twists their minds. She taught me to recognize the numbers - shallow, cowardly hiding behind one another.

"Don't you know", said Dante, "there is no such thing as evil. There's only the absence of good."

I looked at him in surprise. "Wow – you are very deep today," I said.

"Look to your left. There's a cute guy," Dante pointed out to me. "I think he's checking you out."

He was. I smiled back, coldly. Dante and I played this game all the time – observing who looks at the other one when we were in public. We needed each other for this; none of us could figure out by ourselves who likes us and we would never notice any sign of interest if it bit us.

"What's wrong with this one?" Dante wanted to know, seeing my glacial face.

"What, you wanna see me married or something?" I snapped back. "I am not looking for anybody, that's all. I want to be alone."

Love was so simple to me; I had always seen right through it. Getting it was easy enough. Very common pattern, love; found everywhere in shameless directness, waiting to be looked at and awakened; its numbers, always naïve and brave, likeable and joyous, worked in many liberal combinations; even clueless people had a good chance of getting it right.

For years, I had been looking for a love pattern of my own; especially created for me and my hopeless situation; at first, I thought it could be leading me to a man-creature forged in magic fire. But then it became clear that I was looking for something that didn't exist in Nature; she had taken care of that. She had made sure what I was missing was not to be found in this world.

"I have never seen you with any guy, ever," Dante continued. "I know you like guys 'cause I see how you look at them sometimes. I even know which type you like – the tough ones who don't talk much."

I laughed. "That's, like, so not true." I said. "They're all an open book to me, no matter if they talk a lot or don't talk at all. I see right through them. People bore me."

"How can you not like any of them?" Dante asked. "Haven't you ever been in love?"

"Nope," I lied. "Never. And I am pretty sure it will never happen either. You see, I was not built for it. I was built for other purposes."

"What are you talking about?" Dante dismissed me. "Life has no purpose. We're here by mistake and we just wander the Earth and then we die. There is no bigger plan. Nobody built you for anything."

"How about you?" I asked. "Have you ever been in love?"

"Long time ago," he confessed, sighing. "I had a fiancée, Vicky."

"Really?" I marveled. "I never thought you'd be the type to get married."

"I was young," he said. "I still miss her terribly sometimes."

"Why did you break up?" I asked.

"She just left one day," he answered. "I woke up and she was gone; she left a note saying she was leaving me. I never heard from her again. I asked everybody and I looked everywhere but she was gone for good. I heard she might have gone back to Italy where her family was. I don't know. It took me many years to get over it, you know, because I didn't understand why. It's better when you know why, when there's a reason, you know."

It was hard to imagine Dante in love; at the time, he must have had substance, emotions, opinions and answers. He was born a whole being then, and not a transparent shadow as he appeared to me now.

"Did you have a fight the night before?" I asked, because I sensed he wanted to talk about it.

"No, we had a nice dinner at my mom's," he answered. "My mom got out the expensive china, the one with the yellow roses. Mr. Saccas was there, he played the piano for us. It was very peaceful, you know. Like a family. Although Vicky didn't like my mom's rose sorbet – which, I have to admit, is an acquired taste. She felt a bit sick and we had to leave early. But she seemed okay by the time we got home."

"Aaaahh," I said. Mr. Saccas, the usual suspect, had made his apparition again. Amazing how he was there for every worthy event in Dante's life. "First your dad, then your fiancée," I continued. "Don't you think it's suspicious how people keep disappearing on you?"

"What's that supposed to mean?" Dante asked confusedly. "One has nothing to do with the other."

"Honey," I said, "It seems to me that two people you loved disappeared and your buddy Mr. Saccas was there every time it happened. I don't know the guy, but that's how it looks from the outside. You should have a chat with him, that's all I'm saying."

Dante looked at me incredulously. "Mr. Saccas is, like, 85 years old," he said. "He spends his time reading the paper and gardening. I doubt he had anything to do with Vicky leaving me. That is just ridiculous."

"Does he live alone?" I asked.

"Yes," Dante confirmed.

"Family?"

"Not that I know of."

"Friends?"

"Just my mom, as far as I can tell."

"The guy is a fake," I concluded. "Nobody lives absolutely alone for 30 years. What, did he fall out of the clear blue sky? He must've come from somewhere; he must know somebody. He practically saved your life when that truck almost hit you. How come he was there? This is all highly suspicious to me."

"He saved my life a couple more times when I was a kid," said Dante. "I was pretty dumb and got myself in all sorts of trouble. One time I almost hung myself playing with this other kid; thank God, Mr. Saccas saw what was happening and took me away before I completely fainted. He had to give me a mouth-to-mouth and I still remember the smell of his breath – because it smelled faintly of lavender. That's not weird, is it?"

"What? That you remember a man kissing you?" I joked.

"Oh c'mon," Dante smiled. "I was, like, 6 years old."

"All I'm saying is, why don't you talk with him," I said. "He was there all your life – maybe he is the one to ask about your father."

"But I think he moved in after my father was gone," said Dante.

"Maybe he knows some things. Maybe your mom talked with him. Ask him anyway, what do you have to lose?"

"I guess," said Dante. "Although all this memo thing was just a mistake and my dad has nothing to do with the Company. That nice lady who was knitting sweaters was wrong."

But he was not going to give it up; it was clearly marked above his forehead; a path was there, new, shiny, awaiting, with the marks of destiny written on it. He would take it, I had no doubt about it.

"There," I said. "Blonde behind you has had her eyes stuck on you since she came in."

"I'm looking at *that* guy," Dante pointed to the left. "He's completely smitten by you."

None of us turned. We both laughed, finishing our beers. Passing blondes, brunettes, tough guys and shy guys, we

walked slowly towards the bar exit door – two beautiful
people with amazing skin, hair, eyes and teeth, shattered
into a million pieces inside.

--*

When I was with him, the voices stopped. The pain, the
memories, the dull familiarity of every situation – gone.
I was innocent; fresh; silly; blank and easy to surprise. I
didn't know anything. Life would expose itself to me
petal by petal, scent by scent, sound by sound. The
world was smooth and right and I would feel it in my
body, in my limbs, and not solely in my mind.

I met Dan at a party in college; my roommate, a well-
intended, clueless girl, had set me up and dragged me to
a rented barn at the margin of Iasi, where I found all my
classmates drunk and loose, banging their heads to the
heavy metal music. The barn was near the Ciric lake, in
the middle of a frightening dark forest that whooshed
with disgust when it felt me near. I rushed to the middle
of the dance floor, on solid cement, where I was safer. I
smiled; I banged my head up and down with the others.
Metallica music was good; was urban and steely, and
protected me from the angry sounds of the grass outside.

I gathered some numbers, a few, arranged the patterns of
my escape; memorized the paths I could take back to the
car, the times when the forest had to breath and did not
pay attention. And then I saw Dan and he saw me, in one

of the few unplanned moments of my life. Before I could
rationalize it, I was in love. The numbers had fallen into
place naturally, effortlessly, building an almost physical
link between us before our eyes even met. I can still see
it; 10 years later, from the other side of the world, the
link, the bridge, the channel between us looks exactly
the same: the diameter of a young tree; the flexibility of
a bamboo; the lightness of aluminum, the duress of iron;
it is the color of flesh; it starts from my chest and it ends
at his chest, a straight line, wherever we are. I can follow
it and it would lead me right to him. I know where he is
and I know when he hurts. I am chained to him forever,
and grateful for it.

Dan was a true son of Nature. Physical, athletic, he
measured the world by his body's sensations. He took
the day as it came, rain or shine, forest or asphalt, walk
or drive, with the same joy of living. He ate and drank
with a passion, and Nature fed him the best it had. He
was everything, strongly anchored into the tree of life,
laughing at the easiness and beauty of it all.

He came to me, reached for my hand. It fit into his
perfectly. He was my match in every way, my hero, my
hope for salvation. When we danced, I forgot who I was
– for the first time since I had been born. I saw myself in
his eyes: so young, so beautiful, so right; his future
bride. I looked good; I looked normal; I looked like a
woman, like a human being. My aching body was a

whole and not a painful recollection of sick cells and
faulty blood vessels. My eyes were not hollow any more.

I loved him beyond any limits. I still remember his large,
warm hands holding me that night when we danced. I
felt a fire in me that I had never felt before; I wanted to
melt into him, to become a part of the wonderful entity
that he was. He asked me if I'd like to get some air; sure,
I said, let's have a cigarette. We went outside on the
porch overlooking the lake and the waters didn't mind;
the wind was gentle and it played with my hair. The
forest had quieted down; when I was with him, Nature
was kind. I lit a cigarette and offered him one too; we
chatted; we laughed; we kissed. You know, he said, I
don't really smoke. This was my first cigarette ever. I
just wanted to be with you here, away from the crowd.

He kissed as he lived, forcefully, manly, with no
embarrassment or doubt. His lips tasted of exotic leaves
from forgotten mountains; his tongue, always finding its
way inside my mouth with no hesitations or apologies,
felt like fresh oranges yet to be picked. We kissed a long
time; he stroke my hair tenderly, touched my face and
my neck, leaving burning traces along my skin. We
stared into each other's eyes and we knew we have
found our destiny.

He took me home in his car, and we passed through the
sleeping campus, still under our magic blanket of new

love. I live in there, he said, pointing out one of the buildings. My roommate is out. Want to come in?

I had never wanted anything more in my whole life. But then I remembered; it came back to me, the reality I had forgotten for a few hours; who I was; my illness; my inability; my hanging out of the branches of the tree of life. I was surprised and shocked to remember; that couldn't be me. I was a young, beautiful woman in love now; for sure, the nightmare had passed. But then I knew it hadn't.

I can't, I said. I can't. He shook his head, he understood. He was a gentleman. He drove around to my dormitory and took me to the door. A summer rain had started, rushed, noisy. It was a wonderful evening, he said. It was magical, I answered. And so I passed through the glass doors and instantly returned to my Cinderella self, dust and dirt grown on my bones and my mouth, bitter saliva in my throat.

Later that night, I was awoken by the silence. The wind had stopped raging at my window; I heard a knock at the door. There he was – Dan. All wet, panting. I had to see you again, he said. I climbed through the balcony. Please let me in. I can't go to sleep without you. I love you. I love you already.

He kissed me again, rain drops on his lips. Before I knew it, he took me in his arms and carried me to my bed. We opened our eyes to see each other naked, amazed, in love. His body was smooth and strong, his skin sweet like honey. He was the only man I saw naked. He was the only man I ever let see me naked.

You are so amazing, he said. I have never seen anyone so beautiful.

I can't have sex, I said.

He stopped. I'm sorry, he said. I thought you wanted it too.

I do, I answered. God knows I do. But I can't have sex. Ever. I am sick. I don't have the equipment. It's physically... almost impossible for me to have sex.

He got up from the bed, a hurt look on his face. Got a cigarette? he asked.

I don't think he ever really believed me. I think that he always hoped that our love would conquer this small impediment. At times, he might have thought that it was all in my head; or that I didn't love him enough. But I did.

"So you never had sex with him?" asked Lou.

"What kind of stupid question is that?" I barked. "Of course not. We did other things, sure. But I can never have real sex."

"But you've been together for 5 years", Lou wondered.

"And by the end of our relationship, Dan was smoking two packs a day." I said.

We never stopped planning for our wedding. We were so much in love; he had accepted my condition with that fatality of a man who understands that life is sometimes good and sometimes not so good; he accepted the fact that he will never be a father, and yet he still wanted me as his bride. We planned the wedding in detail; the ceremony; the three priests; the location – Voronet, one of the most beautiful monasteries in Romania. It was to be an extraordinary event, and I imagined it as a truce between me and Nature, a unilateral acceptance, now that we shared a precious being – Dan.

Ca la nunta mea
A cazut o stea;
Soarele si luna
Mi-au tinut cununa;
Brazi si paltinasi
I-am avut nuntasi;
Preoti, muntii mari,
Paseri, lautari,

Pasarele mii,
Si stele faclii...

He proposed three months after we met, in the impetuous manner he was making all his decisions. I have never loved anyone the way I love you, he said. If I can only be with you for the rest of my life, loving you, then I am happy. Let me love you, he said. And I did, for 5 years. But I could never bring myself to set a wedding date.

Three years into our love, Dan fell sick and fainted as we were walking down on the Copou Street in Iasi. He recovered immediately and joked about it, but the nausea came back the next morning. A 25-year old, 6-feet man fainting two times in 20 hours was highly unusual. We went to several doctors and Dan underwent several tests; was tested for and cleared of several diseases; in the end, the doctors couldn't find anything wrong with him and had to let him go.

But I knew what was wrong. It was me. I was bad for him, bad for his health, just as I was a danger for any other plant or animal in Nature. I was poison for his soul and his body. As we went along, he lost weight; he was pale. In the mornings, especially after our awkward sex nights, a white powder lay beside his side of the bed; dead cells shed off his body in his sleep. Slowly, his numbers turned into a prognosis of leukemia and death.

"And so I left him", I said.

"Did you tell him why?" asked Lou.

"Of course not," I answered. "Nature was killing him off because of me. Instead of him dragging me into the tree of life, I was dragging him out of it. He was not fulfilling his purpose in life – to be with a normal woman, to procreate. I had to leave."

I chose to disappear one day, quietly, irrevocably. No reason, no other communications with him. I packed and came to America, put the ocean between us. I left no address, no phone number. He suffered for a while, but he got better. Eventually, he forgot me. He was not weak. I was a strange memory from his youth, just another thing that made him into the man he is now.

"A pillar of the community", I told Lou. "Happily married, with four children. Healthy as a horse. Ski champion of Iasi county."

"Wow", said Lou. "Nice job."

"I hate his wife", I admitted. "I hate her so much I could kill her. But I won't. Because that's a chapter of my life that is done and closed."

"I sometimes wish he had died of leukemia." I said later on. "I sometimes wish I had stayed, even if it would have killed him. If he were dead, this would be so much easier to deal with than being forgotten."

"You did the right thing", said Lou.

"Yeah," I said, "like I really have the luxury of being nice. I have to think of myself first if I want to survive. He was my only charity act. And it hurts so much, even after all this time. And I will never do it again. I can't afford not to be selfish."

--*

When Dante got home that evening, a man was waiting for him. He had a briefcase and a suit. He was sitting on Dante's townhouse stairs when Dante parked his car.

"Can I help you?" asked Dante without surprise. Sometimes, women and men would follow him home in adoration and sleep on his lawn.

"My name is Chris Henderson," the man offered, shaking Dante's hand with energy. "I am a lawyer and I work for the Company. Can we talk about your stock options?"

"Well, okay," said Dante. "But I don't have any stocks or anything."

"It's only a legal matter, sir," the man added hurriedly. "Can I come in?"

"OK," Dante accepted. "I gotta tell you though, I figured everything out already about these shares of mine. And my dad's. Yeah, that was interesting."

"I'm sure I can explain everything," said the man as he was entering the house. "We did not contact you because we had express orders from your father since 3 years ago. But now that he's gone and the new CEO wants to take the company public, it all came out of the archives and I understand it must have been quite a shock for you, sir."

Dante had frozen near the door, keys still hanging in his hand.

"What?" he asked. "3 years ago? And what do you mean he's gone?"

"I apologize for using that word, sir," the man answered. "I definitely did not mean *gone* as in *dead*, sir. Everyone who loves him in the Company hopes and prays that he is still alive. Even three months after his disappearance, I'm sure he's fine."

"In the Company?" Dante repeated.

"Well, it's hard to find a better CEO than he was. People really loved working there when he was in charge. And he'd been running that company since it was founded in 1968. He sold the first strategic study ever that year, sir."

Dante sat down on the couch slowly.

"What do you want?" he asked the man.

"I just need your signature here, sir," the lawyer answered. "You are authorized to sign for you father too, as tonight the official 3 months is over and he is formally declared... well, *gone*. He has instructed us to contact you in case something like this might happen."

"Sign for what?" Dante asked, looking at the thin contract.

"For the shareholder's meeting, sir," the man answered. "It's next Monday and you need to sign for the delivery of all the documents about the Company's IPO. You need to do this if you want to vote next week."

Dante didn't want to vote. Voting was very much the last thing he wanted to do just then.

"Okay," he said, signing the papers. "I guess I'd like to vote. Especially if I get to vote for my dad too. He's gotta have some bunch of shares, right-o?"

"Quite a few indeed, sir," the man answered. "49%, as a matter of fact. With your 1% added on, you make it very hard for anything to pass if you don't like it."

"Hmm," Dante nodded approvingly. "Can't say I dislike that idea. What do they do at a shareholder meeting anyway? Can I fire my boss and a guy who tried to beat me up today? I could vote for *that*."

"You can take your place on the Company Board, sir," the lawyer answered. "From there you can pretty much tell the CEO whom of his employees you consider incompetent."

"Wow… In this case, I have to start making a list right away… "

"If you don't mind, I'm going to go now, sir," the lawyer said. "I have to pick up my son from school. My colleague was supposed to be here, not me, but he got himself into some car accident."

"OK then," Dante said getting up and showing him to the door. "Thanks for stopping by. Say, do I owe you anything for stopping by?"

"No need for pay, sir," the lawyer smiled. "Your daddy was a personal friend and I owe him many things. You have a good night now."

Closing the door, Dante took a deep breath. An uneasy
feeling had clung to his stomach. For a brief moment, he
has had a daddy. His daddy thought about him, gave him
Company stock when he was an infant, and left clear
instructions about him to his lawyers. As early as three
years ago, his dad talked about him with this Chris
Henderson guy. His dad pronounced his name – Dante –
when discussing his business with the Company.

Dante held to the thought longer, sweet lingering
sensation under his tongue. He had a daddy.

--*

My uncle Costin lived in the Enchanted Willow forest.
Once renowned for its fairies and gentle wolves, the
forest had become home to a small farmers village and
the villagers' domestic horses and sheep. There was one
fairy left, and my uncle had spent years trying until he
finally managed to sleep with her. He had no control
over himself when it came to women; aggressive, silent,
he'd prey on them the same way he went hunting for
deer. His lust did not wear off easily; he had
complicated, long relationships with women of all ages
and standings; he did not want to give them up, not one
of them; he managed his love life like a business: cold-
blooded, precise, effective.

I despised him as a child; his numbers were cumbersome
and shadowy, curled around his legs and thighs like a

vine. I could not see them well enough. One day, in the dark pantry at my grandmother's house, he slipped his hand down my back slowly, like he was measuring and weighting me. I turned to him and his eyes were blinded with desire. I was 8 years old.

In time, I came to accept him – or rather learned to ignore him. He had nothing to teach me except the dark side of lovemaking, and I had no use for those lessons. His spells were always the same, half light and half shadow, peeking from behind him like hounds waiting to be released.

My uncle had managed to single-handedly destroy the last swirl of enchantment in the willow. The fairy, now old and weak, used to be a beautiful young girl with gracious spells in her hair just a few years before, before my uncle tricked her into loving him. Her name was Eliza. I had met her once, when I was visiting my uncle; I wandered into the forest, just because it seemed so utterly void of feeling. I saw a few crows and a few rats; distorted numbers here and there, marking the path of each dying fairy.

Eliza stood by the small lake. She had long, white silver hair and a deep-green dress. She sat with her feet in the water, her head bent. Her face was shining with a happy melancholy, her piercing black eyes lost in memories. She was the most beautiful creature I had ever seen in my life. Her numbers aligned perfectly – her inner beauty must have matched her exterior one.

"Hi, Eliza", I said. My uncle Costin had mentioned her name, bragging about his new affair.

"You must be Anna", she smiled. "Costin said you'll be visiting."

"What happened to the Enchanted Willow?" I asked. "I hardly saw any signs of life on my way here."

"Death," she answered, sadly. "Death came. We couldn't stop it. We made a mistake, we danced too late."

The fairies appeared to mortals and danced during the Rusalii night – a religious holiday celebrating the descent of the Holy Spirit upon the apostles. Sometimes, they'd be good and show people tricks, like the face of a loved one reflected in the lake; more often, they'd be bad, and they'd steal somebody's food or baby girl; you never knew.

She got up with grace, her dress flowing in the gentle breeze. And then I saw Costin's spells, black cuffs around her ankles; swirling up her pale feet with the cleverness and patience of a wild tiger in waiting.

"You're glowing… You're in love?" I asked her.

She laughed. "Of course not", she said. "I have no heart."

But she was lying – a purple, narrow line coming out of her mouth.

I closed the memory back, softly. That night, in Gaithersburg, MD, all was well. Once more I had witnessed something I chose not to do anything about. To preserve my being; to survive, in good condition; to not disclose the full awe of my powers, for fear I might be spotted and killed instantly.

It was 4:00 AM in Romania, the time when my uncle Costin usually came back from the Enchanted Willow and his fairy lover; he had to – his spells expired at the first light of dawn, and he needed to reinforce them around his house. I've seen him in my Aunt Virginia's memory of an autumn morning. Costin stepped through the dark like a cat, on carefully learned paths. Behind him, Eliza's flower bed trembled in the dim light; Eliza herself struggled to get up, only to be overpowered by the black spells around her neck. She fell back, confused, lost.

"What are you doing here?" he had asked my aunt, with the same harsh tone he had used when they revived me.

"Why didn't you come last night?" she cried. "You said you'll come. I waited for you! Were you screwing the

damn fairy again? Don't you see she's an old hack
now?"

"I hate you so much", my uncle hissed. "You are the
worst thing that ever happened to me."

"Why do you say that?" she whined. "What did I ever do
to you? I always give you everything you ask for. I gave
you my potions, my plants, my power. I gave you my
body and my soul. Why don't you want me anymore?"

He pushed her aside in disgust and continued to walk.
Virginia sat down on the wet grass, tears flowing down
her aging cheeks. He can make you love him, but he
can't undo it, she thought. You're his forever. I'm his
forever. She looked back at Eliza's silhouette amidst the
dead flowers and felt sorry for the poor creature. At least
she, Virginia, still had a family to protect her, but Eliza
had no one. Virginia was never innocent, while Eliza
was a pure being when my uncle seduced her.

My aunt gathered a few stones from the ground and
looked around for wood for a small fire. In silence, she
cast her spells in the morning fog. The willow accepted
and approved with a cold breeze; when the time will
come, when my aunt's love will end, she will let the
forest kill him.

Her love ended that night, as Lou and I were watching
Friends, cuddled on the couch. The death of my

grandfathers changed her and made her face her mistakes; the numbers in the forest needed a slight adjustment to make the fatal spark. A strong, vengeful wind surrounded my uncle as he was hurrying home. He tried to hold on, but the willow had gathered too much hatred. Eliza's voice rose in a horrible scream. My uncle Costin was thrown against several trees before the fatal hit to his head.

By the time *Friends* ended, his memories came to me in a rush - clear, powerful, magical, cunning.

CANTO V

In the beginning was the Word. In the beginning it was
the sun in the deep forest, warm rain washing the stones,
millions of bright stars in the dark beauty of the night.
Nature was a merciful master holding the world in
loving hands. It was balance and, at an arm's length, the
Universe slowly rocked the Earth in its cradle.

My aunt Virginia had green eyes and warm blonde hair;
she was 16 and in love. She would run out at midnight to
meet her lover in the alley behind the high fence; her
white teeth shining through the darkness, her nightgown
like a wild bird. She'd run into his arms, breathless,
beautiful, seeing herself through his love-struck eyes.
Love was a mirror to her. She needed adorers, flowers,
passions and fury; she'd devour and consume love like a
vampire drinking blood, a painful ache that had to be
healed. She fell in love every day, every night; she saw
herself in their eyes and she was irresistible to herself.

Nature accepted her from the start; she was fertile and
healthy, liked to walk bare-foot in the grass, and liked all
animals. She was much more a part of Nature than she
was a part of our family. In the night, Nature would put
soft flowers underneath her body and gently support it
when it came down in the swirl of passion. Small,

yellow blossoms were crawling up her spine, following her lover's hands. Fireflies reflected on her skin as it turned pale and red, dancing to the spectacular rhythm of life itself.

25 years later - lovers reduced to a few, blonde hair getting thinner, skin sagging - my aunt Virginia realized she was more than a body with desires. She sold her 2-floor condo in the midst of elegant Bucharest – place of renowned orgies and parties - and returned home, weary, doubtful, lost. She needed someone to blame, and my grandparents gladly offered her a cause. She became aware of her heritage and her enemy – and hated Nature for not keeping her young and beautiful.

There I was, a card shuffled amongst her memories; my aunt Virginia came running into the house to see me cold and breathless, my grandfather screaming for help. She whisked me into her room; she had potions there. She sat me on the bed while prying open her dresser. She stopped to look at me and the three of us – me as a child, her, me looking through her eyes now – suddenly knew, with a cold chill in our bodies, that I was dead and that it was too late.

Virginia stepped back from the bed and sat on a chair; she was not sad. She felt relief and slight amusement; she hated me, we all discovered. I was the child she never had, the child of her boring sister whom she did not understand. Her sister, sick since childhood, fragile and thin, was able to bear a child; while she, Virginia, wasted her youth and body away.

She did not move for minutes. As we contemplated life, death and suffering, the lateral door opened and my uncle Costin entered the room. A fast, tall, athletic man, he was my father's brother and also his complete opposite. He assessed the situation in a second.

"What are you doing?" he yelled at my aunt. "Save her," he said.

"It's too late," Virginia answered, shrugging. Her voice filled with unexpected emotion, we noticed.

"You can bring her back," he ordered. "I know about your potions, Ginny. You found the hidden Corner Flowers up on Empress' Rock. I know you have them, how else could you have done what you did that night?"

Her heart raced, but she blocked the memory and refused to indulge.

"I have only one left", she said. "And I was keeping it for..."

"Didn't you learn *anything* in over 50 years of living?" he asked. "You can't abuse it every time you need a boost of confidence, for God's sake. You are old. She is young. She is our future. Your one Corner Flower will not keep you alive forever, but she might. It's not too late. Do it."

"No matter the consequence?" she asked. "No matter what she brings back with her?"

"It's still our best chance," my uncle said. "Do you want to live?" he asked, coming close to her, breathing near her ear. She trembled. "Do you want to feel young again? Do you want me to make you feel young again? Do you want it, over and over? I know you do. This child is our best bet, Ginny. Didn't we mixed and matched until the pattern blossomed? Didn't we wait for years until your sterile sister could get pregnant? I want to *live*, Ginny. Without this child, I will die. Do you want me to die? Do you?"

"You know I don't," she whispered. "Am I not allowed to be weak?" she asked, as she got up to look for the potions again. "I have known you since you were a year old. Your pretty blue eyes, your white face. They bred you into this, like all of us. At least I tried to escape, to control. Why didn't you marry Sylvia? Why did you break the pattern? Then you could indulge your power dreams."

"Sylvia didn't want me," he grinned. "We still have choices, you know. She didn't like my pretty blue eyes and my white face. She liked my hairy, dark brother.

The family agreed to her choice; it broke a pattern but it was acceptable."

"Here," my aunt said. "The Corner Flower."

"Do it," he said. "I'll leave by our path. Find me there later – I'll wait." He caught her arm as she was moving around the cabinets. "Bring your potions," he hissed. "Eliza is indisposed today."

She accepted, humbly. She crushed the small, velvety white flower in a stone dish, while he walked away. The emotion left her too, the doubt bringing back old demons dancing in the shadows on the wall. But she chanted anyway. She put the crushed petals on my body and on my forehead. She danced, in a sad trance. As I came back from the dark, she swiftly threw three drops of water on my head. It smelled of roses.

I cried. It was better in the place I had come from. It was warm and forgiving, and lonely. My aunt took me in her arms; at the bottom of the stone dish, the last petal was crumbling. She decidedly took it and swallowed it in silence. Then she walked me out of her room and back to my grandparents.

"Did she bring anything back?" my grandmother asked.

"Doesn't seem like it," my aunt answered.

"Did you use the whole flower?" my grandmother checked.

"Yes", my aunt lied. "I used the whole flower."

But I had brought something back with me – the memories of the dead, awakened in my genes by the unfortunate trip between worlds. There I was: a few weeks old, pale and grave already, as the pain of all people had already started to creep up through my veins, hot and cold, stingy and sour, like a disease fatally embracing the core of my being.

--*

As soon as Dante stepped into his cube on Tuesday morning, apathetic and filled with thoughts about his dad, he noticed that something was off. For one, his computer was gone. And his supervisor was waiting for him inside.

"Hello, Da Vinci. You're late, they're asking where you are", the supervisor mumbled, obviously nervous and distraught for having to speak so closely with an employee. He never remembered Dante's name.

"What's happening?" asked Dante suspiciously. Never in his career had a boss stopped by to bring good news.

"Good news", the supervisor grinned. "You've been selected for the team-building camp."

"Huh?" Dante quipped.

"It's a great honor, Leonardo," the supervisor said. "I would have killed to be selected. They say only those that are being trained for high-power management positions are invited."

"But," Dante argued, "I really don't want to be in management. Can you send someone else?"

Two large guards entered the cube and signaled to Dante to follow them.

"Sorry," the supervisor said. "Valois insisted that you go. Go ahead, enjoy, you lucky guy."

Silenced and terrified by Valois's name, Dante followed the guards to a bus in front of the building. The bus was white and had no inscriptions and no license plate. The guards made sure he got in before locking the doors. The bus departed immediately, almost hitting a row of cars in the parking lot.

Dante looked around himself; the driver had a large black hat that hid most of his face; in fact, Dante was not even sure that he could see anything through that, plus a heap of dirty hair falling on his face.

"Hi," he said, turning to the next row of chairs, where an Asian-looking giant was staring him in the eye. "Do you work for the Corporation too?" he asked, hoping to make friends with some high-powered executive.

"No," answered the giant, and turned his head away towards the window.

"Oh," Dante mumbled.

The bus was carrying about 10 people, all of them men, and all of them completely unknown to Dante. He figured they were probably so high up in the Company's management, that he never had met any of them. He pondered the idea of going around and introducing himself, but nobody else was talking and the driver was rocking the bus pretty badly. It somehow didn't seem like a good idea.

He did notice though that everyone else looked really tall and muscular; like wrestlers or basketball players. Obviously, he thought, it was not the first time they were going to a team-building exercise camp.

Eight hours later, the silence really started to bother him. There was nothing to look at through the windows either, but grass and trees for miles. The last people he had seen were hours ago on a field, an old farmer who looked sick and some other men helping him out. If the

Company was trying a team-building success, then how come nobody even tried to communicate with each other? Besides, the more he looked at the men in the bus, the less they looked like high-powered executives. Dante was almost sure that one of the guys in the back was a janitor in the building.

"Are we going to be back by 5:00 PM?" he asked loudly. "Because I have dinner reservations," he lied – mostly because it seemed the thing to do when all the other guys looked so much bigger than him.

"The camp is for 3 days", the giant next to him hissed.

"3 days??" yelled Dante. "But I don't even have a change of clothes. For God's sake, nobody told me that."

The giant shuddered. Just then, the bus turned a sharp left onto a country road.

"What the heck is this?" Dante asked. "West Virginia?"

The bus rolled over the hills, deeper and deeper into the country side. Unexpectedly, it stopped in the middle of the road.

"Get out!" the driver yelled. "All of you, out!"

Everybody rushed out in silence. Dante, deciding to keep some dignity, walked slowly to the bus front.

"I said, move!" yelled the driver again, and shoved Dante out the door with no mercy.

By the time Dante had regained equilibrium on the ground, the bus had left in a cloud of dust. He looked around; everyone else seemed cool enough. They had obviously been through this before and they knew that the abuse had ended.

"Maggots, assholes, filthy rats!" somebody suddenly yelled at the top of their lungs. Dante turned to see a huge fellow with a worn baseball bat looking straight at him.

"Who, me?" Dante asked with zeal and a smile. He so wanted to not upset this man.

The man ignored him the way you ignore a fly and moved forward.

"Welcome to Camp Hell," he said loudly. "I'm Hardy. You pieces of shit, you deserve nothing. You will learn to be real men here. It is more that any of you are right now. Say 'Thank you, sir' for the privilege of being here."

"Thank you, sir", the men immediately answered, before Dante could join in.

"Do you have a problem with me?" Hardy inquired.

"No, sir, not at all," Dante answered. He could sense the danger in the air, thick like blood. "I quite like you, actually," he added with enthusiasm.

"You Alighieri?" Hardy yelled.

"Dante, sir, " replied Dante. "My name is Dante Portinari…"

"Whatever", Hardy interrupted. "Here, have an egg."

Dante extended his hand in time to catch an egg in his palm.

"Whatever you do while you're here…" Hardy said in low voice, "Do not leave that egg off your sight. Do you hear me? If anything happens to that egg by the time you leave, I'll make you regret the day you were born. Understood?" he suddenly yelled.

"Sir, yes, sir!" Dante yelled back, remembering from some movies that this should be a satisfactory response in this situation.

On the horizon, the sunset was setting in. Dante was cold and tired. And he really had to pee.

--*

In my uncle's memories, his mother was a powerful figure, present almost everywhere. He had adored her. When he was a child, my grandmother would whisper secrets in his ears, aside from his brother. Costin was a beautiful child – blond, curly hair, green eyes, long cheek bones. His brother Marin, my father, was two years older than him and his total opposite – dark skinned, chubby, common-looking. My grandmother did not make it a secret that she loved Costin more; he got all the good food, all the good clothes, all the good games. My father got to do his choirs and sleep in the small guest house with my grand-grandmother, Catrina. She was the one that raised him and gave him the nurturing love he was craving.

When Costin was four, he tried to set fire to the guest house during one dark night. My father awoke in time to stop the flames.

When Costin was nine, he pushed Catrina down the attic stairs. My grandmother laughed loudly at her son's sense of humor; Catrina never fully recovered and died a few years later, missed only by my father.

When Costin was eleven, he made a habit out of stealing small coins from the farmers gathered at the church on Sunday. He'd buy cheap, sticky sugar candy and eat it alone in the garden, hiding from his brother who could have asked for some of it.

When Costin was sixteen, he noticed a beautiful girl who lived across the lake. She had long hair that waved down her back and dreamy, innocent eyes. Her name was Silvia. By then, Costin had learned enough magic to go out on his own. My grandmother had taught him the dark side of spells – the ones that enslave your mind and your body.

His magic never worked on her; it washed right off and never affected her. She married my father two years later, in secret, by the lake. My father had built hidden shelters all across the hills; he was tough and silent and never complained that life had dealt him a bad hand.

"You promised her to me!" Costin yelled at my grandmother.

"I'm sorry", my grandmother replied calmly. "It was meant to be. I tried everything, and I failed. It was just meant to be, they are supposed to be together. It's God's hand."

"There is no God and you know it!" Costin said furiously. "Every time you fail, you blame God. Every time you succeed, you say it was your merit. Don't you see he's just a word for you? One thing you inherited from old senile Catrina."

There was more there; I sensed my grandmother's secret, deeply buried – one secret that she didn't even tell her own son she adored.

"What is my destiny now?" Costin continued, oblivious to his mother's silence. "You promised her to me!"

"I'll find you a good wife", she said. "Don't worry. I'll get you someone healthy who can have children, I promise."

Months later, he married a nice country girl named Flora. She was submissive and humble, not very bright at all. Her youthful beauty wore off fast and in just a couple of years she looked tired and old. She never got pregnant. My grandmother blamed it on God.

When Costin was forty, he learned that my mother was pregnant with me. He came home and coldly poured poison in his wife's food, then watched her die after two hours of suffering.

But it was not her fault. Of all the hundreds of women he dated all his life, none of them ever carried his child. However, he had never stopped trying.

"Why?" he asked my grandmother. "Why?"

"It's on to us," my grandmother answered. "Don't you see the patterns changing when you breathe? It knows…

we are not free anymore. Mother Earth is on to us…
We're a cancer, we'll be exterminated. The whole family
is in a circle of death."

"But my brother had a child," he hissed.

"That child came from God," she answered. "That child
was not meant to be alive, but God gave it to us. Maybe
that child is our savior. She will fight the curse, she will
see through the numbers; she will lead us in the dark.
She will bring a new magic alive, a more powerful and
true one. If you want to live, you better take care of that
child."

"What's so special about her?" he asked.

"She is not human," my grandmother answered. "She is
stolen from Mother Earth herself; she is fertile and
healthy and hears the cries of the wind."

"Of course she's human," my uncle scoffed. "She came
from her mother's womb."

"So did Jesus," my grandmother said.

My uncle did protect me the best he could, as far as I can
remember. He did not believe my grandmother's stories
about God, but it was obvious to him that I had an ability
to cast spells and a capacity to survive unfortunate
incidents. In time, he came to believe that I was simply

the vehicle through which the genes of the family would survive – in the anamnesis, and in flesh and blood. I was the keeper of the family's knowledge, and that seemed important enough to him to defend me. I was his second chance at immortality.

I lay back in my bed, thinking. Lou had fallen asleep, looking like a pale angel. When I was a little girl, my grandmother would whisper stories to me. We'd be sitting in the dark, the flames from the chimney throwing dancing shadows on the walls. My grandmother talked about the lives of the saints; about Jesus and God and the Holy Spirit; about miracles and tragedies. I knew what God looked like; he is painted on every church ceiling in the north of Romania. He was old, kind and patient. He had blue eyes, a white beard and a red-and-blue robe. He was holding out his hand, reaching to everyone who was looking up. But why did He send me into this world?

--*

In a freezing dorm, Dante wondered desperately how nobody missed him. He had no friends, except for Eric and Anna at the office, and no one ever stopped by his apartment to see how he was doing. His mom was used to hearing from him on Saturday afternoons only. It was Tuesday night and not a soul in the world gave a damn where he was.

When Vicky was living with him, a period he
remembered mostly as a blinding white light of sheer
happiness, they checked on each other and protected
each other. She was sweet and shy, and none of them
talked much; but they both liked Dante's chicken
cacciatore above anything and they both ate dinner in the
same tempo, with their feet underneath them on the high
chairs. Dante realized painfully how much he still
missed her; how he was still hoping she would be back;
how he had never let her go from his heart.

He was suddenly hit by the misery of his life – the bad
job, the loneliness; the unresponsive, confusing mother
who never had clear answers to anything; the missing
father, who threw Dante's life upside down with stock
options and corporate meetings nobody prepared him
for; that freak, Valois, who wanted to kill him for no
reason. And all that lead to this moment when Dante lay
naked under a cold blanket in a bungalow, on a field in
West Virginia, sleeping near men who seemed ready to
beat him up all day long. Near his bed, in his shoe,
carefully packed in his socks, was the precious egg.

Getting over his sadness with a deep sigh, Dante decided
to try and sleep for a while. The next day could be much
worse. It was hard to fall asleep when he had no dinner
at all – all they provided was a pile of walnuts and water,
and Dante was not able to get any. He watched the other
men cracking walnuts in their spectacular fists or
between their teeth. Dante tried several methods but

could not crack open even one walnut before Hardy
yelled at them to get out of the dining room.

They stepped outside into a sordid court that looked like
the deserted scene of a village hanging ceremony. Hardy
yelled for a while about different things, trying to teach
them to be tough men. Dante had a hard time being
tough, considering that he had to hold an egg in his
palm. Hardy then went around with a hat with some
tickets in it; they all picked one. Dante's said "Purple".
Hardy made them all say their colors loudly; there were
four color teams: Red, White, Green, and Purple. As far
as he could tell, Dante was the only one in his team.

"Tomorrow," Hardy had yelled, "we'll learn how to be a
team. We'll learn how to fight the enemy – whoever is
not on your team. Survival is the name of the game.
Now move to your dorms. Move!"

At least there were showers, with cold water, it's true,
but Dante could wash before slipping into bed. Hardy
insisted they all slept in the nude.. He said some cliché
about men living naturally. He took their clothes and left
only the shoes and socks. The other men didn't seem to
mind. They all looked amazingly big and muscular, and
comfortable in their skins. However, Dante went to bed
slightly worried about the team fights the next day, given
that he was the sole Purple combatant. That just meant
that he was everybody else's enemy.

Turning from one side to another, Dante could hear his stomach grumbling in revolt. He thought longingly about the precious egg in his shoe. He could maybe sneak back to the dining room and look for a stove, and boil the egg and eat it; maybe there were even more eggs there; maybe there were piles of food nobody knew about. Dante swallowed hard; his feverish brain imagined a glazed ham waiting for him at the other end of the campus; it was pink and crusted with coarse pepper and brown sugar; it called his name lovingly.

He got up carefully, picked up his egg (just in case there was no ham), and found his way out; a dim light was throwing dancing shadows across the court; the stars were numerous and close, like he had never seen them before. He entered the dining hall and blinked a few times, to get his eyes used to the dark; in the back, he saw a door and happily skipped to it. Sure enough, there was a kitchen and a stove, and a fridge, and even a sink.

Suddenly filled with hope, Dante carefully opened the fridge; to his surprise, there was no ham; actually, there was nothing in there except for a pack of baking soda. Dante sighed and returned to his egg; opening the stove, he found a small pot and filled it with water. He dropped the egg in the water and waited impatiently for it to boil. The fear of facing Hardy without his egg in the morning had been overcome by his hunger; Dante didn't care anymore.

"What's up, man?" he heard a familiar voice, and turned around to see Eric. "Whatcha doing?"

"Eric," Dante whispered. "Thank God I see a sane person around. Did they bring you to this training thing too?"

"Yep," Eric confirmed slowly. "Found any booze in here? I need a damn beer, man."

"No, there's nothing in the fridge," Dante answered. "I am boiling an egg 'cause I'm starving."

"I saw some ham somewhere around here, if you're hungry," Eric announced casually. "I think it was in the dining room."

"Show me, dude," Dante rejoiced. "I am buying you a carload of beer when we get out of here."

Dante followed Eric back to the dining room, smacking his lips. Eric stumbled across in the dark and fell against the wall several times. "Whoa…" he admonished himself.

"Where is it?" Dante asked, feeling the dining table.

"Come this way, man," Eric called. Dante followed him to the door and outside the building.

"Oh, *come on*," Dante sighed. "Is this one of your drunken jokes? Where's the frigging ham?"

In the next second, the building exploded in a noisy, shocking bright light that brought Dante face down in the mud. The fire illuminated the whole campus and soon the court was swarming with naked men throwing buckets of water at the dining room. Dante raised his eyes but Eric could not be seen anywhere.

"Are you trying to kill me, Alighieri?" Hardy yelled in Dante's ear, poking him to get up. "What did you do, you moron?"

"Nothing," Dante sworn innocently. "I was just boiling my egg…"

"You did what?" Hardy screamed even louder, pushing Dante back with such force that he ended up back in the mud. "What did I tell you about the egg, you son of a bitch?"

"I was hungry, okay?" Dante screamed back, revolted. "So what, I was going to eat your stupid egg. Fine, I failed the test or whatever. I'll never be a senior manager like these other guys. So what? Nobody was going to promote me anyway."

"It wasn't an egg, you filthy idiot," Hardy yelled. "It was a tracking device. You boiled a $100,000 microchip, you bastard."

Dante shut up. "Oh..." he said softly."Well, I'm sorry."

"You'll have to pay that back, asshole. I'm not gonna take the heat for this one from Valois. I ain't got that kinda money. You have the fancy office job, you pay. You hear me?"

"OK, OK, whatever," Dante said, just so he didn't have to argue anymore. "Can I go home now? Tell Valois that I failed, okay? He can fire me tomorrow and bill me for the egg. I'll pay in installments, okay? Now give me my clothes, damn it."

"Not so fast there, Purple," Hardy pronounced. The fire had subsided and a few naked men had gathered around them. "You left these men without a kitchen and without food. I think this is a darn good theme for our first team building exercise. Get him, boys!"

Dante's instinct took control of his body before his mind did. Before he knew it, he was running for his life, deep into the woods, followed by an angry mob of naked men, who had apparently armed themselves really quickly with tools and sticks from around the farm. He stopped behind a tree when the noises seemed to die down; breathing heavily, with sore feet and quite ashamed of the whole situation, Dante stood there trying to think what to do. In the dark, further south, he thought he saw Eric's drunken silhouette stumbling on the narrow path. "Wait up!" he whispered, hurrying up after him. "Wait up!"

CANTO VI

It was Tuesday night and Dante did not show up for the Wings & Claws beer fest. Tuesdays were especially important because the bar owner, a short, self-absorbed suburban big-shot, was selling half-priced beer taps and giving away stupid prizes to the heaviest drinkers.

I waited for him for a while, and then called him with no result. I left soon after my second beer and it took half of my trip home to finally see the worrisome numbers hanging on me near my left rib. Dante was in some kind of trouble, one far away and hidden from me; one of which I could hardly catch a whiff, a feeling; hardly a foggy sensation in my stomach. A crisp, new number had appeared and it worried me because it meant changes were going on in Nature, in the core and soul of the matter; changes I had to learn, to understand, to spell and defend against.

Caught in the vortex of changes, Dante's destiny had swayed and curled; I thought it might have been me who brought it there, just because I was prone to destroy people as soon as I got friendly with them; but that wasn't it. He was not important enough to me to really matter, or so I thought until then. He was never on the radar as dangerous because he was drinking beer with me every other night.

The warning was weak but unmistakable. As I got closer to my house and further away from the mall, it started to resemble a rapid heart beat and a rushed breath. I scanned my memories and fortunately did not see Dante there; he was still alive. Going through memories of the day, I found an old farmer who had died in the West Virginia fields while working. One of the last things he saw was Dante's face at the window of a speeding bus cutting through the hills. He remembered it vividly because Dante looked a bit like his son, and then the bus became a metaphor for his life hurrying to pass before his eyes. His horse farm had been in the family for four generations at the foot of the Appalachian Mountains. Fastest way there from DC: Route 7 straight up.

I stopped the car in my parking lot and went upstairs to discuss it with Lou.

"Are you crazy?" Lou asked me panicked. "Go and save him, he was kidnapped, for God's sake."

"He's okay," I said. "If they wanted to kill him, they would have killed him already. They'll just scare him, probably."

"He's not like you," Lou reminded me. "He *can* be scared. Just go get him."

"I can't," I admitted. "First, I cannot admit through my actions or words that I am worried or care about Dante; if I do, it's like I'm marking him for destruction. I have to be cold and rigid with him, and then we can be friends, see? Second, how will I explain to him what I am doing there? I would have to tell him that I'm a freak and that I am made of a different matter than he is. There, again, go my chances of ever seeing him again, even if I save him."

"So… You are letting him die because you … are being a good friend?" Lou tried to understand.

"He's not gonna die." I sighed impatiently. "Why would they kill a dumb kid like him? He's got nothing."

"He's got those stock options," Lou remarked.

"I can't go," I said. "I have one real friend in this world and I will not risk that relationship to save him a night of discomfort. If he's not back by tomorrow morning, I'll see."

I went in the kitchen and poured myself a large glass of water. It was cold and it felt good; on my rib, dark-red shadows appeared; there could have been a fire.

Thinking fast, I picked up the phone and called 411. I asked for Mr. Saccas in Arlington, Virginia. Fortunately there was only one listing. I called and said I was a friend of Dante and that had disappeared that day; that I heard him say something about the Appalachian Mountains; that he was supposed to be back but never made it; that I was worried.

Mr. Saccas took the details in a short, calm conversation, with the professionalism of a cop. He thanked me and even spared a moment to assure me everything would be okay. I knew he would rush to save Dante, like he had done so many times before.

I opened the fridge and got a soda; I drank it slowly. I decided that Dante's destiny was his alone. That even though he was also an anomaly of sorts, a transparent, good-hearted shadow I could not comprehend entirely, he and I were different beings with just a few things in common; and that was all. I had other things to do, more important than saving his life – for example, keep looking through the memories of former residents of Gaithersburg and locate valuable information about hidden plants and possible integral corners of Nature, to find the elusive 2-2-9 pattern.

There was a specific place I was looking for in their fragile memories of this life: a small valley at the corner of Shady Grove Road and Sam Eig Highway. Every morning while I was driving to work, there was a light fog there; almost unnoticeable usually, but sometimes dense and dynamic, swirling above the grass. The land belonged to a farm, one of the few that remained in Gaithersburg even after the suburban growth of the past years. The farmer must have had many offers to sell. Large office buildings and apartment complexes were built all around his land; he must have had a very good reason to stay.

The farm house was white and I could easily observe it from the mall at Rio with a pair of binoculars. No one in the anamnesis had any memories of the house; I couldn't even see as much as one person going in or out. The grass would grow in the summer and dry out in the fall, and nobody came out to mow it. I had spent several nights waiting in my car, but I never saw any movements, except for the fog forming at exactly 4:00 AM on summer mornings.

"I'm going out," I told Lou. "I'll go watch that farm again. It's probably the last place I haven't figured out yet in this town."

"OK," he said, preoccupied. He was busy reading *Daniel Martin*, one of my favorite books. I smiled; he had taken my suggestion to read it.

The Rio mall had pretty much closed when I got there; even the geese on the lake were quiet. I parked at the back of Target, on safe asphalt, and put on my binoculars; Nature had to be observed from a distance.

About three hours later, I felt that Dante was completely out of danger. A little while later, two things happened at the same time. First, a car pulled up at the farm; the gate opened immediately to let it through. A light flickered, and a man appeared at the front door of the house. He was 50ish, tall and strong. He waved at the car and helped open the car door. Much to my absolute surprise, out of the car came Dante himself, shaking, dressed in a long coat and nothing else underneath, as far as I could tell. Mr. Saccas poked his head out of the car window, apparently giving some instructions, then promptly turned the car around and left. The gate closed behind him, and by the time I had turned my binoculars around, Dante was already in the house.

While I was dealing with this new information and crunching the numbers and the possibilities, my grandmother's visions suddenly came to me in a passionate rush, filling my eyes with tears and blushing my cheeks; I knew that she had died at that moment, that Nature took her, alone and unprotected. She had struggled by herself, but she was weaker every day, and I did not help. Her love for me, strong and warm like a summer evening, surrounded me. The stories of the saints she used to tell me as a child resurfaced first, colorful and alive. Her last moments were spent in the garden at dawn, where she slipped into the small man-made pool and was swallowed by waters.

I could see her life clearly, although her memories were still coming in flashes and shocks, as her subconscious pulsated while delivering them into the collective bucket, there for other generations to remember. Her secret, which she had shared with me as a child, was that she had faith in God. She prayed every morning and every night, in silence, in her mind, where no matter of any form could reach. She made the potions but believed that God would make them work, and not her magic. And as far as I could tell, he did, because she got the ingredients wrong several times.

"There is no God," I heard myself say to her at 14, a precocious, sad child.

"Of course there is, sweetie," she whispered back. "That's how you were born. You are a gift from God and his angels and our hope and love."

"I see no numbers for God," I said. "Where are they? Why can't I see them? All I see is stupid people and stupid life and how they never learn their lesson. The numbers are about back pain and giving birth and death. I don't see any divine combinations; I don't hear any of the people who ever lived giving me an account of meeting with God."

"When you believe, you'll figure out the numbers," she said. "It's that simple. They look like the moon."

"Then why doesn't he help us?" I asked. "Why do we have to live in fear and hide from trees and flowers and rivers?"

"He is not the enemy." she said undeterred. "He helps in many other ways."

The conversation resonated in me for no apparent reason; nothing else was as powerful. And then I looked up and saw Dante in front of the farm house. This time, he had a t-shirt and some pants on. He sat there, confused, looking at the dark. I put my binoculars on and studied his face – around his ear, curled like a baby's hair, the numbers were spelled out in a moonlit glow.

--*

By Wednesday morning when Dante courageously went to work, his life had changed significantly. Just hours before he was running naked through the woods trying to dodge a murderous mob, after he had blown up a building by boiling an expensive egg. He had followed Eric through the dark forest until they made it to a small house. Dante had knocked at the door in despair and the old man who had answered was so nice to let him in to use the phone.

The man was a woodworker; his tools were everywhere. He took quite a liking to Dante, actually. He lived alone.

He had a white cat he talked with in a tender voice, and a big statue of a suffering Christ on the wall. He gave Dante a raincoat to cover himself, made him chamomile tea and patiently explained the directions to his house from I-495 while Dante hurriedly called his mother and asked her to pick him up.

While Dante and his host were talking about his adventures, someone knocked at the door. Dante cringed with such force that the man took his shotgun from the closet before answering. But it was Mr. Saccas.

"How did you make it so fast?" Dante exclaimed, jumping up and hugging him. "I just called my mom a few minutes ago."

"I was in the neighborhood when she called me," Saccas answered calmly. "Come on, I'll get you home."

As Dante was heading to the door, Saccas whispered something to the woodworker; Dante saw the man kneeling down, a smile on his face, and Saccas quickly helping him get up. "We thank you," Saccas said. "You will not be forgotten."

The road home was filled with Dante's tremolo voice, explaining what happened to him. Saccas listened carefully and approved of Dante's actions.

"Where's Eric?" he asked at the end.

"I have no idea," Dante answered, baffled. "He is just like that, he just disappears all the time. You can't really count on him, you know."

"Oh," Saccas said, understandably.

"Listen," Saccas said, "how about I take you to a friend of mine's house tonight? You'll get a good night's sleep and tomorrow we'll talk about what happened. What do you say?"

"I'd *love* to," Dante said with relief. "I don' feel like going home at all, man. Last night that lawyer came, and now there's a bunch of naked executives looking for me in three states..."

"What lawyer?" Saccas asked.

"Oh, this lawyer who told me my dad disappeared three months ago and he left me some stock or something... I *know* that I have no stock in the Company because I already asked around and they told me it was a mistake. So this is all just like someone is screwing with my head. I don't know - what did I do? Maybe Eric did something and they are blaming it on me. That has happened before for some reason."

"Did the lawyer leave you some paper?" Saccas asked.

"Yeah, some stuff. I think it's still in my car at the office… I was going to look through it, but then they took me to this training camp…"

"OK," Saccas smiled. "Don't worry, we'll look at it tomorrow. We'll figure it all out. Here it is," he said, pulling into a farm in Gaithersburg. "Why don't you just rest tonight, and we'll worry about other things in the morning?"

"Okay," said Dante, getting out of the car, still wearing the woodworker's raincoat. A man appeared at the door and invited him in. Saccas promptly turned the car around and left. Inside, Dante found a comfortable chair and sat down. The man gently patted him on the back, with the same loving look the woodworker had given him.

"You're okay now," the man said. "Please, consider this your home."

Later that night, when Dante took a short walk outside because he couldn't sleep, he saw the man praying between the two old apple trees on the left of the house. Dante kept quiet and walked back inside; but he felt at ease and comfortable, all of the sudden.

When he woke up in the morning, the smell of scrambled eggs and bacon had filled the house. Dante was starving. He rushed to the kitchen just in time to receive a huge plate filled with food from the hands of the good farmer.

"I'm going to leave now," he said when he finished eating, his mouth still full. "I don't have any sick days or personal days left at my company and I can't miss work. I'll call Mr. Saccas later."

"Do whatever you please," the farmer approved. "Please remember that you are always welcome in my house."

Before rushing out to the bus station at the corner of Washingtonian Boulevard and Omega Drive, Dante thanked the farmer again from his heart.

"Anytime," the farmer said. "I mean it, anytime."

CANTO VII

The Company building was quiet and sober when Dante arrived at work. In the elevator, he heard two women talking about a certain Officer Kampf who had had an unexpected heart attack and died the previous day. Dante did not think he knew the man.

He bumped into his shy boss, who immediately backed off and ran into his dark office. Dante sighed and continued through the long, lonely aisle towards his cube. He grabbed a plastic cup and filled it with water. There was nobody in the kitchen, not even the H-1B visa crowd of cheerful Indians who usually traveled in packs around the floor. He passed empty cubicles, the result of all the recent layoffs. Somebody was whispering on a phone close by, though Dante could not locate the voice in the dimly-lit corridor.

On his computer, 214 messages were waiting to be read. Sorting by sender, he deleted most of them. They were company-wide memos and policies that usually changed in the next few days. However, one message was a meeting request from people he had never heard of. Dante looked at the email, puzzled. All he figured was that his boss had signed him up for some useless committee or task force dealing with things he did not care about.

Checking his watch, he realized that the meeting was about to start. The subject of the meeting was something to do with marketing. Hurrying up, he sprinted toward the 5B-009 conference room; no one was there. Dante waited around a bit, looking out the window at the traffic on I-270.

"Can I help you?" a loud voice suddenly broke the silence.

"Yeah," said Dante turning around and looking at the woman who had spoken. "I have a meeting here."

"I doubt it," she snickered. "This is my office now, and I don't have any meetings scheduled today."

"But this was a conference room," Dante replied, confused. "Do you know where they moved the conference room?"

"I have no idea," the woman replied. "Now, if you excuse me, I have work to do."

Dante left the room in a hurry, mumbling an apology. He spent the next 30 minutes canvassing the whole 5th floor, in search of the elusive conference room. He never found it.

He finally gave up and returned to his desk. On the screen, yet another meeting request had popped up – this one, in the Demilune Hall. He knew where that one was – he had passed it just this morning on his way in. It was one of the nice conference rooms built when the Company was founded; when the names meant something real, palpable, like an event or an important notion or symbol. Dante had never been invited to that room – it was usually reserved for senior management meetings.

No one was there either. Sitting alone at the marble table, Dante looked at the oil paintings on the wall; some of them seemed vaguely familiar. A landscape of a farm, a woman and a young boy in a car, down a country road; one of the men in a portrait looked lovingly towards him.

After 10 minutes of waiting in vain, Dante decided to go see Anna. It was already 10:15 in the morning, and he needed to talk with someone smarter than he was and sort out the madness that his life had become.

--*

Dante appeared in my cubicle that morning, looking as confused as he did when beautiful women were tying to talk with him.

"Where were you?" I asked first, closing down my spreadsheet. A slight tension was between us; something that hadn't happen before. We were changed; he was gaining substance and tasting incertitude for the first time; I doubted the numbers behind his head, for the first time.

"God, some really stupid training camp with some executives," he answered. "All I know is that I owe 100,000 dollars now. And today, my stupid boss kept sending me to these meetings, and nobody else showed up! Twice!"

"What?" I asked, pretending to be surprised. As he moved graciously around, it became clear to me that Dante's place had never been there in that cubicle down the hall. It was wrong and unnatural and it was keeping him from fulfilling his destiny.

"Anna, I don't know what's going on," he sighed. "I had such a weird couple of days, you wouldn't believe it… I feel like I am losing my mind."

"You missed last night's beer fest," I reminded him. "I waited for you. Why don't you carry a cell phone, like normal people?"

"Why don't you?" he asked. "I just never needed one, you know. Who's gonna call me? My mom?"

"There's nobody who would call me either," I said.

"I'd call you", he said sincerely, and I believed him.

"Whatever", I shrugged. "How about a cup of coffee at Starbucks?"

I didn't want to lose sight of him again. Events were forming around his palms, extraordinary bursts of cosmic light poking through his fingernails; in the small wrinkles of his face, amazing stories were being written as we spoke. I was a witness to something bigger than everything I had seen before – although it had no definition, no name yet.

"I can't," he whined, "I am out of sick days and vacation days. I shouldn't have taken them when I was just too lazy to get off the bed."

"Then don't take any," I said. "We'll just go for some coffee and be back in a couple of hours. No one will notice that we're gone."

I was somewhat wary of him, I realized. What I had considered emptiness was actually filled with light; what I had seen as weakness, was indestructible. He had escaped my senses for too long; all the things I dismissed about him just turned out to be on a different level from my understanding. The numbers had avoided him, or protected him, to leave him wide open and yet impenetrable to my eyes.

At the Starbucks across the street, I searched for the moon signs on his face while we drank our lattes in silence, feeling comfortable and safe. They were there, a pale aura surrounding his head, and a translucent number behind his ear, hidden in a curl of his hair.

In his future, already taking shape, blurred like a silhouette in the morning fog, a circle was forming. He was becoming round, complete, ripe, whole; his numbers, now brighter than before, were struggling to be round – to give birth to his true destiny, to add up to a one.

I had never seen a 1 being crafted before. People were usually scattered in small, simple equations that blinded and confused them; the numbers kept piling up in their hair and their skin, misunderstood, bringing about old age and disease. To have one number define you meant that you saw above the mundane and the pain; that you defined your place in your time and held strongly to it; that you controlled the details and built them into a meaning for your life.

I added up to a clean 7. I was 14 years old when I finally sorted out the last string of integrations and reached the ladder of harmony. I was exhilarated; no more fractions and crippled data clinging onto my body. Once the path was unveiled, all the numbers fell into place, orderly and quietly. I spent a late night, writing down my feelings as they crystallized into one rational thought; my dreams, as they gained meaning and strength; watched my hand become fluid and smooth, my fingers precise; my eyes clear. And when the change was done, I looked down and saw the number I had been destined to carry: 7.

I was suddenly disappointed and angry at the faith reserved for me; a 7 was a good number but it was not great; the virgin number, which is not born of any others and cannot give birth to any others. In many ways, it was fitting; but I had hoped for a magical 9, or 5, or at least 6. I had hoped for a living, breathing number, one that gets you into trouble but also pushes you to the limits; instead, I got a rigid, cool number that is famous for standing outside emotions and dramas. I re-calculated a few times, but nothing else fit. Late that night, I resigned and accepted my faith. I was a 7.

Dante, however, was effortlessly building a 1. I could have seen it earlier, if only I hadn't mistaken his innocence for emptiness; his transparency for naiveté; his uniqueness for commonality. Yellowish, hesitant, the number of his destiny was taking form behind him, protective, warm; it reached beyond his shoulders, as to encompass and reach others as well.

Somehow, it gave me hope.

"I have to go back," Dante said softly. "I really can't take any more time off, you know?"

"Just let me know if you're gonna go to some camp again," I said. "You owe me a beer and I want it tonight."

"Promise," he said standing up. "Let's go straight after work."

Back from Starbucks, Dante called for the lobby elevator near the Demilune Hall. The old elevator arrived screeching; Dante got in and flashed his badge at the security lock; the signal remained red. He tried a few more times with no result; the elevator doors remained open.

"Is there a problem?" the security guard at the entrance asked him, with a hostile voice.

"Yeah, my badge is not working," Dante replied. "It worked just an hour ago."

"You have to go to the 13th floor," the guard announced. "They'll fix it or give you a new one."

The guard suspiciously worked the elevator buttons, taking great care so that Dante couldn't see what he was doing. "There you are," he said finally, stepping out of the elevator and waving to Dante. "It will go straight to 13."

"Thanks," Dante mumbled as the doors closed silently.

At the 7th floor, the elevator stopped and a nurse stepped in.

CANTO VIII

Nurse Bea hated her name; her body; her hair; her teeth; her shoes; her apartment. Once when she was a little girl, her mom told her that she would always be average: she would look average, she would marry average, she would breed average. Scared, she never married; every morning in the mirror, she tried not to look at her average face.

Nurse Bea loved her white, crisp uniform; her silent office; her metal instruments; her bottles and jars; counting pills. Her job consisted mostly of filing insurance claims. She never had patients in there; if an employee was sick, they would go see the doctors across the street; Nurse Bea's job was to be around in case someone needed emergency care while at work; in the 3 years since she had been working there, that had happened only twice – a couple of days ago when a guard had a fatal heart attack, and a year ago when a janitor felt sick and she had to call Dr. Maygny across the street.

She had received the call two hours earlier; it seemed that a "deeply disturbed" employee was raising eyebrows with his behavior – and could she check him out and see if he was still fit to work?

Nurse Bea felt her heart beating faster; when the guard's heart attack happened, he was already dead by the time they brought him to her office; all she had to do was pronounce the time of death and sign some papers; then they immediately took him away. But a "deeply disturbed" patient was a different matter; she would have to talk with him, ask him questions, get answers; she would have to be alone with him, and she hated being alone with anyone, let alone a crazy person; she would have to maybe even touch him while diagnosing him, and the thought made her sick to her stomach.

Frozen with terror, she sat on her high chair and polished her glass jars over and over again; bouts of sickness attacked her and made her gag; she looked around in order to find a weapon, a defense mechanism, anything that could help her deal with this horrible situation; in the end, she unlocked her drawer and took out a bottle of the strongest sleeping pills she could find.

At 2:00 PM, they called her and told her the patient was on his way; they suggested she meet him at the elevator, as he might be too confused to remember where her office was. Clutching the sleeping pills in her hand, she bravely marched to the elevators and stepped into the one that opened its doors.

She found herself staring with her mouth open; the patient was a tall, handsome man; he was wearing a bright-white t-shirt that showcased his biceps; his eyes were honest and innocent; he looked like he had just come from outside, his hair a little confused by the wind, his cheeks touched by the spring cold. He was the most beautiful thing she had seen in years.

"Howdy," said Dante cheerfully. "Going to 13?"

"Actually," Nurse Bea managed to articulate, "they told me to meet you here and take you to my office. It seems that you have some medical paperwork to fill out."

'Oh," said Dante, "okay!"

He didn't mind following her at all. He peeked at her as she was leading the way; something about her had caught his attention from the moment she stepped into that elevator, even though he could not say what it was. She had short, wavy brown hair and green eyes; she was wearing the purest, whitest nurse uniform he had ever seen; underneath it, Dante guessed the contour of the purest, whitest lingerie he could imagine.

They entered her office and Nurse Bea signaled him to sit down; she calmly filled a glass of water and handed it to him, along with two of the sleeping pills she had in her pocket.

"Take this," she said, opening her palm to reveal the white pills with the letter K on them. "There's a nasty flu going around, we're giving these to all employees."

"Oh, okay," Dante obeyed immediately. He was following her moves with hungry eyes, until he realized what it was that made her so irresistible – she had grace. Every step she took, every gesture she made was soft and fluid, sustained by a subtle elegance. It was a rare quality, Dante believed, and one he had only seen in his mother sometimes. But while his mother could make grace happen when she needed it, Nurse Bea's was natural and clean, coming in waves from her every movement.

"I'm Dante," he said, extending his hand.

"I know," she answered, reaching and shaking his hand.

"Don't you have a name?" Dante insisted, holding her hand into his a bit longer.

"My friends call me Bea," she said looking down, as if embarrassed.

"Bea!" Dante exclaimed. "That's a great name!"

Nurse Bea shrugged. "Let's start your test," she said.

"What test?" Dante asked playfully.

"I had reports that your behavior was unusual these past few days," Nurse Bea said in a calm voice.

"Oh, God, tell me about it!" Dante said. "The weirdest stuff happened to me! They sent me to an executive training camp and then some people wanted to kill me for cooking an egg! There are emails with my dad's name in them! I had meeting requests, and then I'd go there and there'd be no one! I feel like I'm losing my mind!"

"Aha," said Nurse Bea "So, tell me, what do you see here?"

She pulled some inkblots cards from her drawer.

Dante yawned. "I don't know, a tree in bloom or something?" he answered.

"Aha," Nurse Bea said again, and made a note in her notebook. "How about this one?"

"Two good fairies knitting together," Dante offered smiling. His teeth were white and regular, and aligned perfectly between his lips.

Nurse Bea made another note carefully. She had no idea what his answers meant; that was for Dr. Maygny to decide later. Looking at the inkblot, she couldn't help thinking that all she saw was a creepy insect with legs of iron; but fortunately, the test was not about her.

"So who's President?" she asked suddenly, changing her method.

"President of what?" Dante yawned again. He had leaned towards her across the desk, looking her in the eyes with all the charm he could muster.

"Of the U.S.," Nurse Bea said coldly. "Who's President?"

"That would be Bush," Dante said. "What kind of test is this again?"

Nurse Bea was not an expert in this type of thing, but she got the distinct feeling that nothing was really wrong with Dante; he was nice and calm, and she regretted giving him the pills out of fear that he might be aggressive. His beautiful blue eyes were getting smaller by the minute.

"Listen," said Dante. "I had a really bad week. But now I'm glad, because that's how I got to meet you. I'm sorry I never got sick before and needed to come here. Would you like to have some coffee sometime?"

She blushed. From all the men she had ever met, Dante was definitely not average; for a second, she wondered what he saw in her; but she felt guilty for what she had done to him; and besides, the temptation was too great - so she nodded in approval.

"Great!" exclaimed Dante in excitement, and a moment later his head fell heavy on the desk and he started snoring.

Nurse Bea came closer and carefully, slowly, caressed his hair.

--*

I walked through the hallways of shadows and silence; I stepped through the pieces of souls on the floor; I opened the doors where the cold fire was burning; and I was in my office.

I closed the door behind me and sat in the half-broken chair. The artificial light was sharp and disturbing. My office had no windows, but at least it was an office. They had to give it to me when I cracked that algorithm and saved the Company from a nasty virus that had brought our paycheck system to a halt.

My job as a mathematician was so easy I could have done it in my sleep. I hardly had to follow a step-by-step solution to a problem; usually, the numbers aligned clearly from the beginning. I could see through their tricks and gimmicks; they liked to play, to hide, to distort reality and then reveal themselves to me, smiling, bright, like children caught near the cookie jar.

All I had to do at work is pretend I was stupid; take a long time to solve complicated problems, pretend encryption is hard to do. Then I seemed like a normal smart person and everyone was okay with it. My boss, an old man whom I rarely saw, was happy to get my solutions emailed to him and left it at that.

There was a new project in my Inbox. I was supposed to team up with an engineer and come up with the equation that defines lightening patterns during storms. The Company's Weather software was a best seller and they were looking to improve it; as for me, I laughed. I had determined weather patterns when I was four years old and had never seen a computer before; my grandfather could tell weather with a precision of two weeks ahead even when he was too drunk to walk.

I had a deadline of three months and a partner apparently named Feliks, who had wasted no time and had already sent me a meeting request regarding our new project. His name meant "lucky" and it made me smile, for it had shallow hopes attached to it already, before it had even touched the man's life. It must have burdened him as he grew up, as his teeth poked through his gums; that's where the shallow hopes of one's parents live, fester and die.

It was all good; all I had to do was meet with this guy once in a while, pretend I'm working otherwise, and I had three months free to concentrate on my family problems and to follow Dante's saga. To make sure I didn't forget the deadline, I wrote an email to my boss with all the equations and their solutions, and saved a draft in my personal folders, to be sent out at the end of the project.

I was so confident as I walked over to Feliks's cubicle, that I didn't see the crevasse opening before me in the floor tiles; I walked without calculating my movement, my current direction on the curve of life. In my defense, you can't always calculate before you step – then you would never step at all. Each step has infinite possibilities ahead of it, and most of the time you have to just trust that the one with the biggest probability will hold true and the Earth will not swallow you as you put your foot forward; most of the time, the numbers are tame and boring, subdued by the city noise and asphalt, retreated up in the branches of trees in small, curled strings.

I was not paying attention as my soul decided to open its mouth and take a breath of fresh air, come out of the prison where my body was holding it down with heavy chains of fear, disease, and death visions; it lit up in my chest, vulnerable, silly, day-dreaming away for a little while.

"*Cholera jasna!*" I heard suddenly, in a clear, loud voice; it was definitely coming from Feliks's cubicle, the only one in that corner of the floor. I chuckled; I used to swear in my native language, too, when I was pissed off. Feliks was probably Polish or some other Slavic type from some neighboring country back home; I felt friendship for him already, as we shared common ancestors and common legends. The invisible, linking cord between us had begun to form.

I went in, smiling, totally unprepared, and stepped straight into the deep hole that had formed sinuously on my way over, waiting to fool me and trap me; I fell for long seconds and struggled for words to break my fall as Feliks turned and looked at me with honesty in his eyes. I saw it coming a moment too late: the red, fiery dragon I had defeated long ago, now stronger than ever, shattering all in its way to possess me again. There was no time for spells, for barricades, for protection; it curled into my blood and broke into a million sparks and pops. And so, on Tuesday, April 20th (with x pointing up towards Taurus), at precisely 3:42 PM EST (with y pointing backwards to midday), in the most random of circumstances, I fell in love.

"Hi", he said. "You must be Anna." His voice was reassuring and safe. We shook hands and I sat on the spare chair, knees trembling, embarrassed at my own stupidity, shoving back my feelings into the ugly hole they had crawled out of and attacked me.

Feliks was a decent, kind person who took life for what it is; his numbers combed nicely around his smooth face: deep but not dark, interesting but not wild. He was a wholesome 4, a practical Earth sign, with healthy genes that were striving to breed and survive. Some early, minor tragedy had shaped him into an introverted, almost solitary person. I scoured for leftover numbers in his aura; there were some bad feelings, some unlived fantasies I could have used to make him love me back; there were good chances that I might ruffle and confuse enough numbers around him, to make him want me.

Beyond the rigid pattern he was born unto, beyond the equation that defined him to the world, his soul was shining through, warm and beautiful; he had so much love to give, a whole mountain of golden, brilliant gifts meant for the one he hadn't found yet. I wanted it so bad to be me.

--*

When Dante opened his eyes, he saw Bea's worried face hovering above.

"Oh, you're up!" she exclaimed. "Thank God. I thought I killed you."

"I'm okay," Dante said weakly, looking around. He was lying down on the narrow bed in the medical office. "So what happened?"

"I gave you a bigger dose of medicine than I should have," Nurse Bea confessed, hands frantically wringing. "They told me you might be dangerous."

She looked so cute in her perfectly pressed white uniform, with her cheeks flushed from embarrassment, that all Dante could do was to smile large and gesture dismissively with this arm. "Don't worry about it," he said, getting up slowly. "How about that cup of coffee? Then I promise I'll forget this whole thing."

"I... I could use some coffee," she said blushing. "Besides," she added professionally, "I was just going to suggest you have some. It will help the medicine wear off."

"Great!" Dante said, standing up on his two shaky legs. "I think I can walk to Starbucks from here."

She hurried to help him and he gladly accepted, leaning on her even though he could have probably made it on his own; she had a small body frame that felt even smaller when he put his arm around her narrow shoulders; her hair smelled of lavender. He inhaled blissfully, half closing his eyes, and together they walked through the glass doors of her office.

"I'm not feeling so well," Dante said when they got to the lobby. He was a bit dizzy and his stomach was nauseous. "Maybe I should take a rain check on the coffee. I think I'll just go home."

"Oh, no," Bea protested. "No way you can drive like this. Please, let me drive you home. It's the least I can do."

"Sure," Dante agreed. "Can we please take my car? It's been here at the office for a couple of days and I'd hate to leave it here again."

"No problem," Nurse Bea said.

Dante gave her the keys and led the way to his car. "It's in Alexandria," he said, snuggling into the passenger seat. "Just make a right here on Washingtonian and then take GW Parkway. It's pretty close."

By the time Nurse Bea got in the car and put her seat belt on carefully, Dante had fallen asleep again. She hesitated for a moment, then turned the key on and made a left on Washingtonian. Scared, worried, and somehow happy, she drove to her own apartment.

--*

"Feliks made the funniest joke today," I told Lou that evening, all agitated and unable to find a place to settle.

"Sit down, for God's sake," he said annoyed. "You're making me dizzy. Who the hell is Feliks?"

"You shouldn't swear, kid," I said, sitting down on the couch. "You're too young for that. Feliks is this great guy I'm working with."

"I haven't heard you use the words 'great guy' in, like, ever." Lou said, bringing about the tea cups and the honey.

"I know," I said. "Pretty pathetic, but I like this one. And you know what, I think he might like me a little too. He was looking at me when I wasn't looking at him, you know? That hidden look, when guys kinda measure you up?"

"You mean he was checking you out," Lou said coldly.

"Yeah, I think he was, yeah," I said cheerfully. "And I was wearing that low-cut camisole. Isn't that cool?"

I jumped up and stepped into the powder room. "Look," I said, pointing to the mirror, "I looked good and my boobs looked good!"

Lou got back up and went to the kitchen. I followed him in there, all flushed.

"Oh come on!" I said. "What am I doing so wrong? Aren't you the one that bugs me about never going out with a man?"

"This doesn't feel right," Lou said. "There's something amiss here. What is it that you're not telling me?"

I went back to the couch and covered myself up with the blanket. I sighed. "He's getting married. In two months."

"Oh, God," Lou rolled his eyes. "There are 10 other men who call you and ask you out and you say no… and you have to destroy this guy's life?"

"Okay, first, you are very nasty today. What the hell is your problem? Second, I'm not going to do anything with Feliks. Not a thing, not a date, not a flirt, nothing. You know that I don't have any use for a man in my life. I'm sorry I like him, but I do. Can I just enjoy his company for a while? He's really funny, you know. And so smart."

"You're right," said Lou, taking my hand into his. "I'm sorry. I just had a bad day. Things are changing for me and I'm not sure how or why. There's times when I can't get here anymore, and I'm lost. The path is harder and harder to find. There's fog, and strange noises. Maybe my time is up. I don't know."

"I'm sorry," I said, stroking the back of his hand. "I had no idea. But you know that you'll always be in my mind even if I can't see you anymore. You are part of my memories, you know. You are not forgotten."

"Your memories will die with you – and then it will be like I never existed," he said in a matter-of-fact tone.

"Lou, listen to me," I said. "All of us who lived have left their mark on this Earth. They are all burned inside the next generation, all their knowledge and thoughts, and emotions. It's called anamnesis. It's our spirituality, what we get from our ancestors. We might not know their names, but they left traces inside of us. I am just one who can see these traces clearly; but nevertheless they exist in each and every one of us. You know that."

"But when you die, no one will see me clearly anymore. I will be a grain of sand on a beach. I lived for only 17 years. I never knew much. What do I live behind?"

"Come here," I said. He put his head into my lap and I kissed his forehead. "You made me happy and kept me company, and you've been a true friend for three years. I love you and I need you. You are sweet and caring and you help me live my horrible destiny. That's what you did. You're now burned into my soul. And before I die, I will accomplish my dream and I will leave my knowledge into this world. How, I don't know yet. But I will, because I can't let my gift go to waste. I can't let my family's discoveries be forgotten. So don't you worry. I'll find a way."

He sat there in silence, his blue eyes blurry. "So do you really like this Feliks guy?" he finally asked.

"Like a stupid schoolgirl on her first crush," I admitted.

"Do you think he's the one for you?"

"No," I said. "I don't think there is such a thing. He's earthly and healthy and doesn't believe in things he can't touch. If I get close, I'll just make him sick and unhappy. So I won't. I'll just sit here and love him for a while, that's all. It will pass. It always does."

"Don't wear your low-cut camisole around him then," he said smiling. "You'll drive the man crazy."

*_*_*

Dante opened his eyes yet again to see Bea's beautiful face. "We have to stop meeting like this," he said.

She laughed. She had changed her uniform for a pink t-shirt and slacks. She wore pink bunny rabbit slippers and Dante looked at them, fascinated; they had long ears and whiskers and everything. He had never actually met an adult person who wore anything like that.

"I made fresh coffee," Bea offered. "Please drink. Please don't fall asleep again. You should try to stay awake for a while."

Dante gladly accepted the hot cup for her hands. They touched fingers and he couldn't help notice her tiny, transparent nails, beautifully polished.

"Oh, this isn't my apartment," he suddenly realized, looking around.

"Sorry," she said. "You fell asleep before giving me your address, so I drove here to my place. I hope you don't mind. I want to keep an eye on you anyway tonight. You shouldn't be left alone."

She was a bad liar and Dante smiled, flattered. "So, tell me about yourself," he said. "I mean, if we have to stay awake, we can at least make some interesting conversation."

"Sure," she said approvingly. "Uh… I am from Richmond. I am a nurse. That's pretty much it."

He laughed. "God, and I thought *I* hated to talk about myself," he said. "At least I describe my life in about 10 words, you only used 8."

"It's just nothing interesting, that's all," she blushed again.

"No boyfriend? Husband? Former husband? Come on, you gotta give me something. Look, I'm falling asleep again, see? You need to keep me entertained."

She laughed again. "No boyfriend, no husband, no former husband. I have a major fear of commitment."

"Oh my God," Dante said approvingly. "Commitment sucks. I *so* get you."

They looked at each other, smiling.

"What else is one of the worst things I should know about you?" Dante asked. "Tell me now before we get to the good stuff."

"I am invisible," she confessed after a hesitation. "Nothing happens to me, ever. Nobody notices me. Which is totally fine by me," she hurried to add.

"I have the opposite problem," Dante sighed. "*Everybody* invites me to lunch, I don't know why."

She knew why. In the light of the fading sun, Dante looked like a male supermodel at the height of his career; his arched eyebrows, his turned eyelashes, his strong cheek bones, his honest blue eyes, his tender expression – Bea found it hard to believe that he was actually a real person, illuminating so much beauty around him. She touched his hand gently to convince herself he was there on her couch. Dante immediately caught her fingers and held them tight, and slowly took them up and kissed them.

"I love your nails," he whispered. "So few people know how to take care of their nails."

She enjoyed his kisses on her fingers; instinctively she pulled closer to him, until their hips touched; they both felt the heat, the chemistry swirling through their bodies. Dante turned his attention to her face and gently took her head in his palms, and kissed her trembling lips. She tasted of honey and strawberries, and he could feel her passion underneath all that neat surface, waiting to be discovered and brought forward.

"One last thing you should know about me," she whispered. "I'm a control freak. Hence the perfect nails."

"I was hoping you were," Dante whispered back. "Control freaks are the best."

They kissed again, incapable of keeping apart.

--*

Wednesday night I met Dante at Wings & Claws for
beer; to my surprise, he was not alone – a cute girl was
holding his hand.

"Hey, Anna, this is Bea," he announced loudly as soon
as he saw me.

"Really great to meet you," I said, shaking her hand. "So
are you guys on a date?"

"This is one continuous date we had since we met,"
Dante explained, laughing. "Yesterday she called me in
her office and I fell asleep from the flu pills! She took
care of me last night and then we took today off and just
stayed at her place… and then it was time to meet you,
so here we are! By the way, we're both control freaks,
neat freaks, and we both hate commitment!"

He was so changed; he was happy and excited. His aura
sparkled with pops and crackles; he was in love. I
smiled; the numbers seemed to have fallen in the right
place around him; she completed him in many ways,
enough to keep him interested and comfortable for many
years to come.

They had ordered cheese fries and were eating them in
the same manner, cutting them in small pieces with a
fork and knife held in the correct position as suggested
by Miss Manners; when Bea spoke, she politely covered

her mouth so we wouldn't see bits of the food in her mouth.

I reached and grabbed a fry with my bare hand and bit into it. As far as I knew, that was the normal way of eating those in a bar. But Dante and Bea missed the point I was trying to make. They were too preoccupied looking at each other.

"So, Bea," I said, my mouth open while I was still chewing a piece of fry. "Why did you have to call Dante into your office? Is he sick or something?"

"Oh," she said. "The Manager of Security called me and said Dante's acting weird, and that he needed a head test. But then I don't think there's anything wrong with him."

"Well, of course not," I said. "He just had a bad week, that's all. Lots of unusual things are going on at the Company. That shareholders meeting has made everyone crazy, and all those layoffs – now half the floors are empty and creepy."

"I know," Bea agreed. "I will file a report tomorrow and say he's okay." She turned and smiled at Dante.

"Well," he joked, "it's good to get confirmation from an expert that you are okay in your head."

"I'm no expert," she blushed.

"You are the best expert ever," he said playfully, "Yes, you are."

"Hi," I heard suddenly. I turned around and, to my great surprise, I saw Feliks.

"Hi," I said. "What are you doing here?"

"Just hanging," he said.

I introduced him to Dante and Bea, and noticed that Dante was winking in my direction as if he figured out what Feliks meant to me. I looked back at him with an annoyed expression, and he responded with an innocent face.

"Please join us," he told Feliks. "We'd be delighted."

I looked at Dante again, but he was doing it because he didn't want me to feel lonely while he was enjoying Bea's company. So I didn't say anything and slid over a chair to Feliks.

He sat down and held his own in our drunken binge, downing bottles with that Eastern European good-natured ability to get wasted at any time for any reason. He and Dante hit it off right away; Feliks had a sense of humor and a natural charm that made him irresistible to anyone. Dante appreciated a male friend, and soon was

babbling with Feliks about wars and battles in the
Balkans, things I never knew Dante was interested in.

As for me, I noticed that I could not get drunk that night.
It took all my concentration to pretend there was no
other feeling there except friendship – which I really felt,
too, but was overcome by a burning desire of holding
him against a wall and pressing my body against him.
My brain was so busy with all the pretending, no amount
of alcohol could get through to it. At times I talked too
much, in a rush to explain myself to him, to make myself
look interesting and intriguing; but most of the time I
was quiet. Nothing was to come out of this; the despair
was silencing me.

Feliks was not a big talker either; he listened really well,
which was part of his charm. He wasn't as good looking
as Dante, but easily equaled Dante's success with
women; I saw them every time watching him with
hungry eyes, talking to him in softened voices. He was
just above average in height, had dirty blonde hair and
common brown eyes; and yet he had a charisma that
made people notice him as soon as he stepped into a
room. It was hidden in the numbers around his neck, a
string of unexpected prime numbers in an otherwise
ordinary setting; it was almost like an accident, like that
glow and light got there by mistake and could have
disintegrated at any time; but I have seen too many
accidents like this, and came to believe it was them that
made us who we are.

He did not talk much about his fiancée; he also stayed late drinking with us and never called her to say when he'd be home. I saw these things and was satisfied.

In my head, I talked with Feliks all the time; I called him *žabo*, and told him about my life and my troubles; I fantasized about him saying that he didn't care, that he wanted me anyway; to just hold me and grow old with me. That he would die for me and not regret it; that a year with me was worth more than a lifetime with his fiancée.

At home, I dissected this love thing over and over again. It was a different feeling this second time around, much stronger than it was when I was very young; it had powerful roots and many branches and full-blown flowers and large leaves and it knew exactly what it wanted. This love had dignity, nuances, shadows, sweetness and bitterness in just the right amounts; it was mature and painful, and real.

It added a glow to the world, it painted brilliant shadows over my existence; it gave contours and meaning to old things; it made life smooth and manageable, an easy flow under my fingers. It vibrated under my skin, making me smile for no reason; it itched with silent desire. The numbers mellowed, sweetened, lit up all around me; I could sense happiness somewhere close, and I understood what other people felt when things went right.

"So how's your love muffin?" Lou asked as soon as I got home, with an amused twinkle in his eyes.

"So darn cute and so darn smart, I could just eat him up," I sighed. "Can I at least kiss him? I think that a kiss can't do much harm. Come on! What do you say? I'll die if I don't kiss him soon."

"Out of the question," Lou said seriously, shaking his delicate hand at me. "First you want to see, then you want to smell, then you want to touch, then you want to taste, and next thing you know you'll burn in Hell forever."

"I didn't know you believed in Hell," I said, surprised.

"Believe?" Lou asked. "I think I've seen it a couple of times, when I missed my way in the fog."

I laughed. "Why would I be forever condemned if I kiss a man who's not even married yet? Is your God that cruel and revengeful?"

"He's not *my* God. He's just God," Lou said. "If you can't see Him in your numbers, it doesn't mean that He's not there. Maybe He's the one that created the numbers."

I laughed again, bitterly. "The numbers are nothing but Nature," I said. "Little fireflies in the darkness and mystery of creation. And by creation I mean simple chemical reactions that freakishly resulted in highways, marketing strategies and computers as the human race evolved. We're born, we live and we die, and that's it and nothing more. That's Nature, baby. She's all we've got."

"Then what about me?" Lou asked. "I don't have any numbers around me. I am not Natural. Don't I exist? Am I not here in your kitchen?"

I paused. "Are we talking about this now?" I asked. "Because last time we did, you wound up crying for an hour, and I was so upset I couldn't see any numbers the next morning and I couldn't go to work. Can I just enjoy my forbidden love and share my stupid feelings with you, and just hang out here without explaining away the Universe?"

"Alright," he muttered. "But I exist. I don't know why or how, but I know that I am. Just so you know. No numbers to hold me up either. Just me, whatever that is. Just so you know."

"I know," I said, and took his arm as we walked together into the living room. "I know."

Dante spent Wednesday evening at Bea's again. After
she cooked dinner, perfectly aligned noodles of
vegetarian lasagna, he decided to call his mom.

"I didn't go home for two days," he explained. "Usually
she doesn't call me anyway, but I thought after that night
I called from West Virginia, she hadn't heard from me
since and she might be worried."

Bea smiled approvingly. A man who loves his mother
was healthy and normal, as far as she was concerned.

"Mom?" she heard Dante say on the phone. "What?...
Why?... Yes, a lawyer came a couple of days ago... I
don't know, Monday or so... Yeah, but the papers are
worthless, I researched and Dad is not a shareholder... It
was all a mistake, they told me... Yeah, I have them,
they're in my car. Well, but I have plans tonight... Yeah,
it's a woman... Well, I don't wanna... I'll be there
tomorrow night, if that makes you feel better... I
promise. I'll be careful."

He hung up, a puzzled look on his face. "My mom wants
me to go sleep at her house tomorrow night," he said to
Bea. "She is afraid that someone is after some stupid
papers a lawyer gave me by mistake. She thinks people
are following me and stuff."

Bea listened, concerned. Dante had told her his story and it did seem too strange to be just a series of coincidences. Bea was a big fan of conspiracy theories; most lonely nights, she would cuddle up with a mystery book.

"I think it's silly," Dante said. "Why would anyone want some papers with no value? My mom is just being weird, that's all. She's always trying to tell me what to do and scare me away from people and stuff."

"Well, bring the papers upstairs and let's look at them," Bea said. "Maybe there's something in them that you didn't notice."

"I don't see why not," Dante said. "I'll be right back."

While downstairs, he also moved the car to an empty space on Eye Street. Bea's apartment was in Adams Morgan, one of his favorite DC neighborhoods; however, the street parking allowed time was only two hours before nightfall. Searching through his trunk, he found the file the lawyer gave him. Crumpled along with it, he saw the letter he was supposed to give to Valois.

"Oh my God," he told Bea breathlessly when he got back in her apartment. "I forgot to deliver the letter to that freak who wanted to beat me up."

"The Marketing Guy?" Bea asked.

"Yeah, the one who was supposed to know all the Company's history. What do I do?"

"Let's open it," Bea offered. "I don't think you should see him again, and maybe we'll find out some secret about it from the letter."

They opened the letter together. It was a memo addressed to all Senior Management, and it announced the new secure Intranet for their eyes only. It contained an URL, a username and a password for access. Before he even finished reading, Dante had opened Bea's laptop and connected to the Company's VPN using the credentials from the letter. He opened the Intranet home page, and they both stared at the screen.

The web page had a black background and bright red letters. It had links to CPR Reports, Payroll and product development tracking. More importantly, it had a link to the Company's History, which Dante followed. An index page with several other hundred links opened.

An hour and a half later, due to Bea's organizing skills and analytical ability, they were able to summarize the whole history of the Company. It had been founded by Dante's father; they could not figure out the year, because it seemed to have existed forever in one form or another, operating under different names at different times. An Italian company long ago, it had come to

America by the way of New York City, selling olive oil and Italian wine.

In 1968, his father took new partners – Dante's mother and some angel investors from her family, and went public, issuing shares to both partners. Her family name was French – Beaufort. A year later, when Dante was born, they put shares in his name also. From there, it seemed to have sparked a quarrel between partners; there were hostile bids, board coups, and the stock price suffered. In the end, Dante's father had bought back all ownership of the Company, and proceeded to extend its scope and goals until it became universal. His father remained CEO and President but never appeared or used his name publicly; he avoided the press; his representatives were lawyers and PR people. Three months ago, after Christmas, a new CEO with a French name had taken over. Soon, he replaced the whole management with his own people.

"I wonder where my father is," Dante said, worried. "I think I was right, and he really needs me to find him and rescue him. Those French guys only tried to stop me by giving me bad information. I can't believe I wasted three days because of them."

"We'll find him, don't worry," Bea said, taking his hand into hers. "I'll help you, and I'm sure Anna and Feliks will help, too, if you ask them. They are your friends."

"Wait, this is all making sense now," he said, trying hard to think. "They changed the management but not all the workers; that's why I got the memo from the good secretary. But then as I went up the chain, they were erasing all traces of us from the system. When I got to Valois, he was Senior Management, so he knew who I was and he tried to hurt me."

"But why?" asked Bea. "There's a new CEO now. Why do they still want to hurt you and your dad?"

"My brain hurts," Dante complained. "This is hard! Now, if I was a nasty CEO and the former CEO and his son still owed half the company, what would I do? Get rid of them, of course. So maybe they got rid of my Dad. But how come they didn't get rid of me three months ago?"

"Maybe they didn't know about you," Bea offered. "I mean, you didn't know your own Dad ran the Company. Maybe he kept it secret and they found out about it when the lawyer came to give you all the shares."

"So then they sent me to that camp to kill me, yes," Dante agreed. "And when I escaped, they sent me to those meetings that didn't exist."

".. And then they sent you to me. So they're trying to say that you're crazy so you can't use your shares and vote at the meeting on Monday."

"Oh, my God," Dante said. "You are so smart! Yes, this makes perfect sense now!"

"It's probably suspicious if they make you disappear also," Bea said. "First your dad, then you, this would have triggered some nasty SEC investigation."

"What the hell are they voting for in that meeting on Monday anyway?" Dante wondered. He went back to the laptop and clicked on some more links. "Ah," he said, "here it is. Shareholder meeting – oh, they're voting on the new CEO. He's only acting CEO right now. So, yeah, I can see why they're pissed."

"Okay," said Bea. "Here's the thing. You own half the Company. I don't think you should go back to work until Monday. I think it could be dangerous. We'll stay here at my place. I'll call in sick the rest of the week and stay with you."

"Well, I feel kinda stupid hiding out. And quit my job? I don't know, it's just weird."

"Look here," Bea said, looking at the other papers Dante had brought up. "Your dividends went into a trust account all these years. Now you signed this so the account is opened to you."

"Okaaay," said Dante.

"Sit down, baby," Bea said, taking him to the couch. "You have forty-five million dollars in the bank."

"Huh?" asked Dante.

"You are a millionaire, baby," she said softly. "You don't need to work anymore."

Dante thought about that for a minute. It didn't make him feel any different.

"Whatever," he said. "I'll still want to work. Okay, maybe now I can get a job that matters for once. When you think about it, it's silly that you have to be rich to get a job you care about."

"So what shall we do?" Bea asked, sitting down on the couch near him.

"I don't know," he said, putting his arms around her. "What if they come here and hurt you because you didn't file that report that I'm crazy? I can't just hide in here, I feel like a sitting duck. We need to take some action of some kind, now that we know what's going on. Like, what do I do at that meeting on Monday anyway? How do you vote? I don't know any of this shit."

"You need to learn how to be rich," Bea said. "That's okay. Let's sleep on it and tomorrow we'll do some

Internet research and find out what these meetings are and what you need to do."

"Okay," said Dante. "But how do I even start to find out where my father is?"

Bea thought about it. "How about asking Anna? From what you tell me, she is, like, a math genius. Maybe she has some ideas. Besides, she's worked in many divisions at the Company."

"Okay," he said. "I don't know how I would have gone through all this without you. I feel like I've known you forever."

"Me too," she answered. "I feel like I've been dead and now I'm alive again because of you."

They whispered sweet nothings in each other's ears; their love had rapidly grown into a tree and filled up the small apartment, its leaves heavy with promise and happiness.

*_*_*

I spent Thursday with Feliks again, shoulder to shoulder, alone in the Sensibility Lab of our Company's Weather Center. I watched him work his way through formulas, and gently directed him when he was going down the wrong path. He was smart and a quick learner, and he enjoyed being in charge, so I let him.

We didn't have to be there; we both knew that. We both could have worked from our cubicles, emailed back and forth, and we would have achieved just as much. But we had come in that morning, logged into our IM, and almost in the same second sent a message to each other that we should get together and work in the lab. Yeah, he wanted me too.

"You wanna get some lunch?" he asked around noon, stretching his arms and his back.

"Uh… sure," I said. "You're not sick of me yet? We've been here for four hours," I added.

"Nah," he said, dismissing me with one big flap of his hand. "It's all good. So tell me," he said getting up and gentlemanly opening the door for me, "Where are you from in Romania?"

"Small town up North," I said, brushing against him as I was passing through the door, my skin in a state of ecstasy when we touched. "Nobody's heard of it."

"What's it called?" he insisted.

"Cimpulung," I lied, giving the name of a near-by town. I was afraid he might go on the Internet and do a search

and come up with freak stories about my relatives,
especially my uncle who had made his mark in the town
– and not in a good way.

"What's that mean?" he asked, not letting go.

"Long Field," I said dryly. "It's a small town, really. A
miners' town. There's nothing fancy there."

But there was. There were Nature-made wonders like the
three rivers' Delta and the white mountains and the
forests that changed colors all autumn long; and man-
made wonders like amazing painted monasteries. And
then there were wonders made by my family – such as
the fountain in the middle of the town, a sacrifice that
had to be made to the forces that balance, so the town
would be spared from the big earthquake in 1974. It was
a place as amazing as any other, with 700 years of
history behind it; with kids, mothers and fathers, uncles
and grandparents; with life pouring out and holding out
and clinging to the sky.

"Where were you born?" I asked back, as we walked to
the deli across the street.

"Plock," he said. "You know it?"

"Weirdly enough, I've heard of it," I said. "It's got the
Friendship Pipeline, right? And it has a port and all sorts
of cool ruins?"

"That's the one!" he said enthusiastically. "Great city. You should visit!"

I laughed. "I don't like to travel much," I said. "Takes too much planning. Too many possibilities of taking the wrong turn."

"Taking the wrong turn can be good sometimes," he said cryptically. "The planned route may get boring after a while."

A look in his eyes and I knew he was talking about himself, about being stuck in a relationship that was good but not great; there was some discomfort, insignificant maybe but enough to keep him wanting something else, something he could not define just yet; but as much as I wanted to, I could not help him.

"Boring is good," I said decisively. "Boring is perfect. Boring is happiness. Boring is reality. Don't believe in movies – change and freedom are overrated."

He looked at me surprised but didn't comment. We stepped through the deli's doors and sat in line to order sandwiches.

"Don't get the ham sandwich," I told him after checking out the stale, low-hanging numbers above the meat drawer.

"Why not?" he asked.

"I saw that waitress sneezing near the ham," I lied.

"Oh, okay," he said cheerfully.

The man in front of me started to stare at me all of the sudden. I was used to it; I stared back with a blank look. He was wearing a good suit and looked like one of the many financial analysts that worked at the investment company in our building. These guys were worse than construction workers; they would comment to me every single time I passed by. They had huge egos and thought they could have anything with their money; their pick-up lines were pathetic.

"Hi," he said, undeterred by my facial expression. "Couldn't help hearing what you said about the ham."

"Oh, God," I said rolling my eyes. "I was just joking. No need to sue the waitress or anything."

"Well, I can't sue her because I'm not a lawyer," he said, laughing too hard at my stupid comment. "But I can definitely ruin her retirement options."

I didn't say anything and looked unimpressed, hoping to end the conversation. No such luck.

"Can I buy you a cup of coffee with your sandwich?" he asked me, coming a step closer. I could smell his cologne and his skin, and it made me sick.

"No, thanks," I said, stepping back and bumping into Feliks.

"You shouldn't be waiting in line anyway," the broker continued. "You're too pretty for that. Why don't you sit down at a table, and I'll bring you everything you need?"

"I believe the lady said no," Feliks said from behind me, and put his arm around my shoulders. "Now back off."

The man looked confused for a moment. "Sorry," he said to Feliks. "I didn't realize…"

"Whatever," Feliks replied and pretended to whisper something in my ear. I blushed and softened, feeling his breath on my neck; he touched my ear with his lips, and I knew that the inhaled the smell of my hair, and that he liked it. I pulled away with an effort and turned my eyes away.

"How do you deal with guys like this all the time?" he asked me as we got out of the deli, sandwiches in hand. "I mean, you probably have to fight them off with a stick. How does it feel to be so good looking?"

"Oh, please don't," I said. "That's not the only thing I am and I hate it that I am so and I wish my parents hadn't spelled out these features when they were scouring the depths for a baby," I blurted out.

He looked at me confused, probably starting to see that I had problems beyond fighting men off with a stick.

"It's good to be good-looking," I said smiling, trying to lighten up. "People give you things all the time. And they invite you to all their parties. And even if you don't go and you treat them badly, they will keep giving you things and inviting you to their parties. They're just *that* stupid."

"A-ha," he said. "Sorry if this upsets you, you know," he added, "but you are gorgeous and I'm not going to lie to you about it because I'm your friend. You just can't deal with it very well, that's all."

"It's not that," I said. "It's just that there isn't an end to the means. It doesn't lead anywhere. It's not a beauty that brings me love or happiness – so what good is it to me?"

"Why not?" he asked patiently, and I could see him trying to pull the puzzle apart, to understand me, to label me safely in one of his engineer mind's drawers.

We were back in the Sensitivity Lab. We sat down and unfolded our lunches on the spare table.

"I'm just complicated," I said dismissively.

"Well, of course you're complicated," he said jokingly, "You're from the Balkans! We're all very deep people, not like these Americans, right? Must be because of that *rakija*, huh? Gives us all a lot of complications."

We both laughed. "Thanks for helping me with that creep out there," I told him warmly.

"Anytime, *kochanie*," he answered softly, and he meant it. "Anytime."

He bit into his sandwich and looked the picture of everything I was missing – health, sparkle, love, laughter. I swallowed my tears along with my tuna salad on rye.

--*

Thursday morning, fresh and bright, Dante decided to go see his mother. He had slept like a baby and he didn't know if it was because of Bea's loving presence next to him, or because he had realized that he didn't have to go to work in the morning. He hadn't known how much he hated his job until then; he never thought he had a choice. That's what people do: they wake up, they shower and they go to work in a dark cubicle at the end of the aisle, with an invisible boss who spits out thirty memos a day, until the rules and policies pile up all around them, entrapping them forever. Dante had never met people who didn't work, although once a rich lady talked with him at the bank and invited him in her limo but he refused out of his usual displeasure of invitations and approaches from strangers. If he liked someone, he was going to introduce himself and strike up a conversation and ask that person out for coffee; that was his philosophy. Only he never liked many people.

He turned to Bea and smiled. She was making coffee, carefully moving around the spotless kitchen. She looked brilliant in her pastel blue robe, her face lit from the inside by unexpected happiness. She smiled back at him.

"I'll go see my mom," Dante announced. "I have to ask her about all this stuff."

"Okay," Bea said. "You want me to come with you?"

He thought about it, but a new gut instinct he never had before told him to say no. It was coming out of his new love for her, and out of a desire to protect her; he also remembered Vicky and her sudden disappearance after she had met his mother, and made up his mind to keep the two separated for as long as he could.

"No, it's okay," he said. "But I was thinking that you could maybe call a lawyer or something and set up a meeting for this afternoon, and maybe they'll tell me what to do. Also, I'll have to call that bank with all my money and set up an appointment to see what's up."

"I'll make the calls for you," she said. Dante liked that she never used silly nicknames like lovers do. "You take care and call me if you feel sick or whatever."

Dante sipped from the coffee cup she had brought him, perfectly black French Roast coffee that he had grown to love more than any other coffee in the last two days because it was her favorite. "I will," he promised. "Don't go back to the Company without me," he advised as he was getting up. "Those French people might be asking you about me, and maybe you'll get in trouble. And you know what, I'll take those papers with me to show them to my mom. Maybe she knows something about them."

It was raining even harder outside and Dante circled the block three times trying to find his car. He was sure he had moved it a few spaces the night before, but all that medication had left his memory blurry. Wet and cold, he went back to Bea's apartment.

"I can't find my car," he shouted from the hallway.

Bea rushed to him. "I left mine at the office," she said. "How about taking a cab? There's a taxi station at the corner of Columbia."

"Okay," he said. "I know it's there somewhere, I just don't remember where I parked it last night. I guess I was still confused from the drugs or something."

He went back downstairs and hailed a cab from the street.

"Arlington," he said. "Just take Route 50, I'll give you directions from there."

The driver looked at him a few times through the mirror. "Do I know you?" he finally asked Dante. "You seem very familiar somehow."

"I don't think so," said Dante. "I really don't know many people."

It was 7:30 AM when the cab pulled in front of his mother's house. It was a bit early, Dante realized. His mom was probably just getting up. He picked up the *Washington Post* from the lawn and opened the door using his own key.

"It's me, mom," he shouted entering the living room. "I'll make the coffee, take your time."

"Oh, hi, honey," his mom said and came to meet him, surprisingly dressed up already. "I already made the coffee. I'm so glad you came, I was worried about you."

She looked out of the bay window into the driveway. "Did you drive?" she asked. "Where's your car?"

"Oh, I took a cab," he answered, taking off his wet jacket. "I couldn't find my car this morning, I parked it some place last night and I don't remember where. Maybe they towed it or something."

His mom shook her head but didn't say anything. "So who's your new girl?" she asked.

"Oh, just a girl," he said dismissively. His instinct again advised him to keep his new love under wraps, maybe until it was strong enough and mature enough to defend itself against anything. "But I came for something else. Guess what – it turns out all these French people from the Company were after me because I own stock and stuff."

"Really?" his mom said.

"Yeah, Dad gave me a bunch of shares when I was a baby, it turns out nobody knew and now I am a millionaire. Yeah!"

Lucia sat down at the breakfast table, her face concentrated but not as surprised as Dante thought it should have been.

"How did you find out about all this?" she asked, looking him in the eyes.

"A lawyer came to my house with some papers and I thought he was wrong, but then at the Company they found my name as a shareholder, even though the new CEO was trying to delete the records."

"Do you have those papers?" Lucia asked.

"Yeah, I brought them with me," he said. "I was going to ask you to look at them, maybe you know something about all this. I don't know what to do with them, and Monday there's some meeting where I'm supposed to be but I have no clue what to do there."

He leaned to take the papers out of the inside pocket of the jacket, when something caught his eye on the front page of the *Washington Post*.

"Oh, my God," he said. "There's a picture of me in the paper. *Man Disappears Amidst Concerns ForHis Mental Health*," he read stupefied. "What??"

The article quoted Dante's neighbor and good friend, Lee, saying that Dante hadn't come home for four days. It also quoted a co-worker, Danny, saying that he had been with Dante at an executive training camp and they had become friends but Dante acted very weird, then ran away naked into the woods. The article also mentioned

Dante's manager expressing his concern for Dante's mental health, given that the last time he had seen him, Dante was on his way to the medical office for a psychological evaluation. The article then gave a phone number to call if anybody had any information regarding Dante's whereabouts.

"Who the hell is Lee? And Danny?" Dante wondered loudly. "I don't have a neighbor named Lee. This is all a damn lie. I'll call the paper right now and tell them I'm here and I'm sane."

"Don't," Lucia said, grabbing his arm. "What if they send you to a mental hospital? You said it yourself, some bad people are after you. Why don't you stay here with me, no one cares about an old lady. They won't come here."

Dante sat down again, confused. This was too hard for him to figure out. He had spent his life taking the main road, being boring and bland; nothing ever happened to him, except for the hoards of strangers asking him out for lunch at any given time of the day.

"Mom," he said, "look, you know I'm not very bright. But you have to talk to me. You never tell me anything. I want to know everything – how did you meet Dad? Why did he leave? Was your last name French? I always thought you were Italian, like Dad was. Did you know that Dad was the real CEO of my Company? Did you know I had shares? I need to know these things, it is driving me crazy."

"Your Dad never told me anything either, dear," Lucia answered. "I had no idea about the shares, and I had no idea he was a CEO. I truly thought he left us for good or that he died. I'm sorry but there's nothing much to tell. I met him, I loved him, I married him, we had you, then he left us with no explanation. It's very painful to face, but what it comes down to is that he didn't love us enough to stay. There's no conspiracy, just a common drama."

Dante sighed and took his hand in his palms. "I don't know what to do," he said. "I think that Dad is in danger. I think these French people did something to him, like they tried to do to me. Only they didn't know about me until that lawyer gave me all my shares because Dad had disappeared. And I got lucky and escaped them so far. But how do we find Dad? Where do we even start looking, Mom?"

He looked at her over the breakfast table, trying to see if she would come closer to him and hug him or at least hold him. But she was never into that touchy-feely stuff.

"It's going to be okay, baby," Lucia said with her usual tone of voice. "Here," she offered, "I have these pills my doctor gave me. They calm me down and help me think straight."

She reached for the bottle on the kitchen counter and took out two white pills. Dante extended his palm to receive them, but his eyes popped out when he looked at them: the pills had the letter K engraved on them – the same ones that Bea had given him and knocked him out for 24 hours.

For once in his life, Dante had to think fast. Why would his own mother want him to sleep for 24 hours and lie about it? Why was she more interested in his papers than in saving his Dad? Why did his fiancée leave him the next day after meeting his mom? Why was she keeping secrets from him?

His first instinct was to throw away the pills and get out of there, and back to Bea's love and care; but the curiosity held him on the chair. Maybe this was his chance to finally understand who his mother was - and implicitly, who he really was.

He calmly got up and got a glass of water, then pretended to take the pills while discarding them in the sink along with the remaining water.

"Okay," he said, turning back to her, smiling. "I feel better already."

She nodded, preoccupied; she was looking at his shareholder documents, which she had taken out of his jacket. She read in silence, with no emotion showing on her face.

"Uhhhh," Dante yawned theatrically. "I am so tired, maybe I'll lay down a bit on the couch. I had a really rough week."

"Sure, baby," Lucia said absent-mindedly. "Take your time, relax."

Dante pretended to fall asleep after a few minutes; he breathed regularly and closed his eyes, but all his other senses remained more alert than usual.

"You asleep, *cara*?" Lucia asked after a while. He didn't answer.

Lucia went back to the dining area and called someone on the phone. "*Il est ici*," she said softly . "*Oui, j'avais… Bien. Bien.*"

Dante felt the knives of betrayal gnawing at his insides. His own mother was going to sell him to the nasty French people; what did he mean to her? he asked himself. He was a millionaire now, and yet she was still selling him out; he had a good girlfriend, and yet she wasn't happy for him; he loved her, and yet she was lying to him for 30 years.

He was about to open his eyes and confront her, although he wasn't sure what to say to her. But he knew he had to get out of there because he wasn't safe. He thought about Bea and felt warmth and love flowing over him, covering his wounds, making him whole.

Just then the entrance door popped open violently and Mr. Saccas stepped in. Dante closed his eyes back, his curiosity more powerful than his anger.

"Amelie," Mr. Saccas said. "What are you doing, woman?"

Amelie?? Dante thought, amazed.

"I'm doing what I have to do," his mother answered back in a rough, deep voice he had never heard before. "The Company has to return to the rightful owners."

"How are these Frenchmen rightful owners?" Mr. Saccas asked. "They only have a vague connection to your family, and your own relatives didn't want to help them. Besides, this was Christian's company from the beginning of times – and that is not a metaphor. It's his foothold. It's how he does good things."

"He gave me half of it," she said angrily. "And then he left me. I fucking deserve the whole thing for putting up with him."

"These guys will not give you anything, Amelie," Mr. Saccas pleaded. "They are simply using you because you hate Christian. Don't sacrifice your own son for some money. You have enough. Christian sends you money every month so you don't have to worry about it."

"Yeah, all he gives is money," she answered. "How much is he paying you to keep an eye on Dante and me? Now he's paying Dante. He wasn't there when he grew up, no, that was beneath him. But he gives us all money, and we should all be happy and love him for it. Christian doesn't know what good is and how to do good to his own family."

It was then when Dante stood up, incapable of keeping silent anymore. Both Saccas and Lucia turned to him in surprise. Saccas was the first to gain back control of the situation.

"Good, you're up," he said to Dante. "Get your stuff and let's get out of here. Thank God I have her phone tapped."

"You piece of shit," Lucia hissed. "Thirty years I've waited for a chance to get back at him. And you, his paid servant, will not let me have it. After you claimed to be my friend."

"Not using his son, no," Saccas said. "Dante has no fault in this. And, if you ask me, neither does Christian, except that he made the mistake of marrying you."

"I loved him," she screamed, trying to hit Saccas. He fought her back easily.

"You are incapable of love," he said, taking Dante by the arm and directing him towards the back exit. "Good luck with your French buddies."

A shocked Dante followed Saccas out on the back porch and into a car parked on a street beyond the garden. He was holding his papers tight inside of his jacket. The rain had stopped temporarily, but the clouds were still hanging low and heavy.

CANTO IX

I woke up in the middle of a bad dream, sweating, breathing hard. My love for Feliks had grown chaotically all over my fingers and toes; it was poking at my skin from the inside, burning me, making me toss and turn at night. It brought back all my demons, my denials, my anger at the world; it made me think of suicide, kidnapping and murder; it made my despair appear of cosmic proportions, and it made me abandon all hope.

I needed to know more, I decided. I would simply approach this like a project at work, have a plan, and stick with it. I just needed more information so I could make a good plan, I convinced myself. There had to be other people like me who lived before; there had to be other women with this rare deformity, and maybe one of them had found a cure. I had looked for answers many times before in the anamnesis, but this time, I convinced myself, I was more mature and I knew more. I could maybe see a clue, a detail that had escaped me.

I never needed props to start the journey; the abyss was right there in front of my eyes, calling with millions of pained voices. It wanted me, and I wanted it. I belonged there, and it felt warm and safe to me, like a womb; but I

also knew its embrace could steal and keep my mind
prisoner forever, unable to function, frozen in madness.

I thought of Feliks and his handsome silhouette that
morning in the computer lab, his broad shoulders under
the brown jacket. I concentrated until I could remember
every detail of his face, and I painted it in light strokes,
to guide me, protect me and to get me back. I took a
deep breath, closed my eyes and let my mind wander
where the sun was silent.

The voices started immediately, loud and demanding of
my full attention; flashes of light and shadows
surrounded me, but I just kept my mind's eyes on Feliks'
face and did not look left or right. Because I already
knew what was there; lost souls who could not find their
way back into Nature; angry, lonely, feeling let down by
whatever gods they had believed in; the losers, the
cowards, the traitors were repeating their story over and
over, trying to convince me of their good intentions – as
if I had any powers to help them.

Past the angry, loud mob, there were others; some had
been a little bad, some had been a little good. No one
was innocent. No person had lived a perfect life.
Everyone I have ever heard or felt in the anamnesis had
something to apologize for. People had been gross and
stupid forever, and I was happy I was not like them; I
was superior in so many ways and if only I could create
my own descendants, my own race, we would

genetically dominate the planet in four generations. We
would never complain and beg for help, trapped in
limbo; we would contain Nature for good and live the
healthy, sanitary existence in which our minds could
expand the most.

I followed Feliks' smiling face all the way down the nine
circles; lost souls offered to sell me their knowledge, all
of it, and it would just be available to my conscious
mind if only I bargained with them – but I had nothing to
bargain with, and neither did they. I already had their
knowledge since I was there, and they were open books
to me; they were part of my soul and my mind already.

There was nothing new I could find; I desperately
wished for all people to be dead, so I could see all that
they knew at once, so that I could see the big picture,
understand all angles, and be able to devise a plan for
my family's salvation. My guide hovered over the frozen
lake, then turned left and listened carefully. I followed
its eyes, and it led me to two souls which had recently
arrived.

They let their stories be known to me immediately, with
relief. They were from my small hometown in Romania,
and I stopped for a second to find my Mom and Dad's
faces in their memories, to see how they looked now.
Both men had been shepherds up on the Rarau
Mountain; they were out with their sheep when a
powerful storm had unexpectedly started. They tried to

herd their sheep back to the shack but some were so
scared they ran down the ravines, crazed. One of the
dogs chased them and disappeared into the woods as
well. The sky went dark and the wind picked up. The
shepherds hid inside their small cabin and propped the
door closed. One of them lit a gas lamp and put it on the
table; in the flickering light, the Empress' Rock
appeared larger than usual, casting a sharp shadow over
the valley. It came as a great shock to them when a
lightning bolt loudly hit the old rock, splitting it in two
halves as easily as if it were butter. One piece fell over
the shepherds' cabin, smashing the walls in and killing
both of them.

The memory was intriguing and I studied each detail
they remembered. Because the Empress' Rock had been
my Dad's secret hiding place; his favorite spot for
gathering spells and small miracles, and keep them
locked for when needed. That's where he once had
found a wounded winged creature and nursed it back to
life. That's where the rare Corner Flowers were growing
for the well-being of our whole family.

And suddenly I saw it clearly, a vision taking shape out
of small or unspoken details. Nature had destroyed the
Empress' Rock because its defense had gotten weak
lately; as my family was getting smaller, our collective
powers were getting smaller as well. My Dad lost spells
and equations in the storm; if I looked carefully, I could
see the numbers disintegrating into rain drops and

breaking into a thousand pieces when hitting the ground. I could feel my Mom and Dad getting weaker by the minute; around me, lost souls enacted my vision on the Cocytus lake, in a desperate dance, and I knew, I knew with certainty that my parents would die the next day and their bodies would float lifelessly in the Prut River before the sun even reached midday.

--*

I called my mom after midnight, when the day was just starting in Romania.

"Did you see it?" I asked abruptly as soon as she picked up the phone.

"I did," she answered calmly. "I'm sorry, *puiule*. We will be gone soon and we'll leave you all alone in the world."

"I'll have you in my mind, you know that," I said. "I have Grandma and uncle and aunt. They all told me how I came to be like this. It's okay, though. You did what you had to do."

"What about the 2-2-9?" my mom asked. "Any chance of finding it? Any chance of having your babies and saving our genes?"

There was no more time for lies or vague answers.

"Remember that truck that barely missed me when I was 3?" I said. "It didn't kill me, but it crippled me. I can't have any children, in any way. I tried, I went to doctors here. There's nothing they can do."

"Oh, my God," my mom said. "Why didn't you ever say anything? How could you have hidden this so well?"

"I couldn't take away your hope," I said. "I kept trying to find a way."

"Find the 2-2-9," she said. "They say it can make any wish come true."

"I wish I were with you right now," I said. "I wish we could take Dad and all go visit the stupid park in the delta, without fear of roots coming out of the dirt to pull us in. I wish we would have a picnic without being surrounded by protective spells."

"We will, *iubire*," my mom said. "We'll all meet again and we'll have that picnic. We will wait for you by the Delta, and Dad will make grilled *mici*, and your grandfather will boil the corn. We'll be there waiting for you. You just come whenever you want, *iubire*. If you want to give up this fight, I want you to know that it's alright with us. We love you."

"I know," I said, choking back tears. "Let me say hi to Dad."

"Hi," my Dad said. He sounded tired and old.

"Hi, Dad," I said. "Did you have the vision, too?"

"Yes," he said. "Both of us did. It's going to happen tomorrow." He sounded resigned.

"Is there any way to fight it?" I asked, but I knew the answer to that.

"No," he said. "We don't think we should. We think it's enough."

"Okay," I said.

"I prayed for you today," he said. "I went to a church, like your grandma always bugged me to. It's nice. It's quiet and there's no danger. There aren't any numbers except the ones people bring in. I lit two candles for you. I hope you will make the right decisions."

"Grandma told me to think of God, too," I said. "I never paid much attention to it, what with all the surviving I had to do on a daily basis." I sounded angry, I realized. "He could have helped me a little if He really existed."

"We now believe that He does," Dad said. "He is the one keeping the balance between our humanity and our animal nature. But you will have to discover it on your own."

"I promised Grandma I'd keep an open mind," I said.

"*Bine*," he said. "Kisses, baby. We have to go and finish up our business here on Earth. It's been too long. We'll see you on the other side."

"I love you both," I said, but Dad had hung up already.

I cried silently, still holding the phone. Lou came and hugged me with his frail arms, giving me as much warmth as a man dead for 47 years could give.

--*

Dante sat quietly in the car while Saccas drove on I-270 towards Gaithersburg. He took the Sam Eig Highway exit and soon pulled into the farm where he had bought Dante a few nights ago.

"You'll be safe here, son," he said softly. "Come on, let's get inside. It's starting to rain again."

Dante followed him inside the house, where the old farmer came to greet them.

"So happy to see you again," he told Dante, with a slight bow. "Please, make yourselves comfortable."

"Dante," Saccas said after Dante took off his jacket and sat in front of the chimney. "We need to talk, son. Where have you been the last two days?"

"Oh, God," Dante remembered. "Bea! I left her all alone."

He turned to Saccas and grabbed his arm. "Please, go and bring her here. I'm afraid something will happen to her."

"Calm down," Saccas said. "Who is she?"

Dante explained what had happened and how Bea was supposed to set up all his appointments. Saccas listened carefully.

"Call her," he said when Dante finished. "Tell her to go to Café Sofia, it's close to her apartment in Adams Morgan. I'll pick her up from there in an hour. Tell her not to talk to anyone until I get there."

"Okay," said Dante, suddenly understanding how serious this game was.

Bea answered the phone in her usual sweet voice, and Dante felt tears of joy in his eyes when he heard her.

"Love," he said, "are you okay?"

"Well," she said, "there's been some excitement downstairs. A car was being towed and then it exploded right down on Eye Street. They closed the whole area while they're investigating. I think they're finally done now."

"Listen, I'm sending a friend to pick you up. I am worried about you and I want you to be here with me. Be at Café Sofia in an hour, and don't talk to anyone else. My friend is an older man, with short white hair and a grey coat."

"Okay," she said, trusting him all the way. "I made your appointments for tomorrow morning, at the bank and at a law firm here in D.C."

"Great," Dante said. "I'll see you in a bit."

Saccas waved at him from the door and left immediately. Dante waved back, tired and hurting inside.

"Tea?" the farmer asked softly, politely.

"I don't know," Dante said. "What can you drink when you discover that your mother doesn't love you? And that your father is hiding from you, even though you work in the same place?"

"Your father loves you very much," the farmer said. "I know that for a fact. I have known him all my life. He loves every creature, great or small. How could he not love his own son? And your mother loves you in her own way, too. She raised you, didn't she? She is just mad at your father and sometimes she sees him in you. You look so much like him."

"I do?" Dante asked incredulously. "I don't even know what he looks like. There aren't any pictures of him."

The farmer laughed softly. "There are pictures of him everywhere. There is one right here," he said, pointing to the wall.

Dante raised his eyes and found himself staring at what appeared to be a very old icon, painted on red wood. The loving face of a kind man starred back at him; around his head, there was a saintly aura. For a moment, Dante thought he recognized something familiar in it; but then, his rational mind took control.

"Who is that?" he asked suspiciously.

"That's him," the farmer said. "That's your daddy."

"Oooo-kay," Dante said. Obviously, he thought, the farmer was crazy. "Thank you very much," he added, remembering a Romanian saying that Anna once told him: don't argue with madmen and children, it won't get you anywhere.

They sat in silence. The farmer got up after a while and bought some more tea, then spent a while carefully cutting cubes out of a big chunk of cheddar cheese. He arranged them on a plate and added crackers before offering them to Dante. Dante thanked him again, two times in a row, but hesitated to touch the food. He wasn't hungry and felt uncomfortable alone at the farm with an insane host.

The farmer didn't talk anymore; he started up a fire in the chimney and then lit up the two lamps in the room. Outside it was raining again and it was getting dark, even though it was only 3:00 in the afternoon.

Saccas and Bea arrived at last after another hour, and Dante bolted out of his seat and into Bea's open arms. The hugged like they hadn't see each other in weeks; they both smiled happily, like nothing else mattered but the fact that they were together.

"We'll all stay here until this is over," Saccas declared.

"Until what is over?" Dante asked.

"The shareholder meeting," Saccas said. "I'll take you there on Monday, and that will be that. All you have to do is vote against the acting CEO. Then they'll back off and go back in the hole they crawled out of, to cook up more evil plots for the years to come. But it will be over for a while."

"But I have those appointments tomorrow," Dante said.

"You don't need to go," Saccas said. "I'll explain to you what do to. You can go to the bank after the meeting, your money will still be there."

"How about my Dad?" Dante asked. "What if he's in danger?"

"He *is* in danger," Saccas confirmed. "But I'll take care of it. There are still many good people left who will give their life to save your dad. You should stay here where you're safe."

"Do you know where he is?" Dante asked hopefully.

"No, I don't," Saccas admitted. "I have to make some calls, maybe someone saw something. And I wanted to ask you about your friend Anna."

"What about her?" Dante asked, surprised.

"She called me that night you were in West Virginia. I don't know how she knew that you needed my help, but maybe she can help us find your dad."

"Really?" Dante asked. "I had no idea. She always jokes about how she is Romanian and in Romania all women are witches."

The farmer looked uncomfortable but didn't say anything.

"Well, we'll ask everyone we can," Saccas concluded. "If they are good people, they will help us. Now, let's have some dinner. I am starving."

--*

Friday morning I met Feliks in the Sensitivity Lab; we greeted each other quietly. This time we didn't even IM each other – we just both showed up there. When I got in, he was already sitting down at the main terminal. I sat near him, our knees almost touching. Our numbers mixed with small purrs of satisfaction, curling around each other and adding up to a whole new feeling. I pulled back, jerking my being out of his warm reach.

"So what's up?" I asked, trying to keep my voice cool.

"Well, you tell me," he answered dryly. "What exactly is your agenda here?"

I looked at him, surprised. "What do you mean?"

"I found this email you wrote," he said, pointing to the screen where the Company Eye had opened my Inbox and parsed through my files. "It has all the formulas we've been working on. And it's dated three days ago. How did you know this stuff? I hadn't even showed you the weather program then."

"What the hell are you doing reading my email?" I asked furiously. "Who made you my boss? Are you spying on me, are you crazy or something?"

He blushed violently, but his questions were more important to him than admitting he got caught. "I just wanted to see…" he started, and didn't know how to continue. We sat there looking at each other with passion and anger, in one of those classic Eastern European flares which lock eyes and bring all the dirty laundry out in the open.

"Okay, I'm sorry," he said finally. "I like you. I wanted to know more about you. You're sending me mixed messages. I'm sorry I read your email."

"You are crazy," I said. "Don't spy on me, I hate those fucking stalkers."

"How did you know the formulas?" he asked again, undeterred.

In retrospect, I know I could have come up with a few good explanations. But that moment was true and real, and we were sitting close and staring at each other without blinking, and his face was right there and his narrow lips moved and I followed their shape, fascinated; he said something but I didn't hear him anymore. I leaned suddenly and kissed him on the mouth, a simple kiss, and before he reacted I ran out of the room and into the grey hallway, where the numbers followed and surrounded me like a waterfall and reminded me his taste, to enjoy forever.

I rushed outside and into the garage to my car to go home and think about what I did; as I was crossing the lobby, I saw an older man looking at me.

"Anna?" he asked.

"Yeah," I said, scanning him. He seemed alright.

"I'm Saccas," he said, extending his hand. I shook it. We measured each other with our eyes for a while, trying to figure out who the other was. Nobody in my memories ever remembered Mr. Saccas. I couldn't place him; his numbers were not shifting but stable, in a way that only old age and wisdom brings up. He probably didn't know what to make of me either. But we had many things in common – we cared for Dante, and we had strange abilities. In the end, we smiled at each other, recognizing a partner.

"Nice to meet you," I said. "Is Dante in trouble again?"

He laughed. "I was hoping you could help him out."

I could see that he did; there were long strings of unknown variables piling up on his back. He needed me, and so did Dante. I nodded approvingly and followed Saccas to his car, Feliks's taste still on my guilty lips.

*_*_*

To my surprise, Saccas drove straight into the farm I'd been watching from afar for months. I didn't say anything, but noticed its glow and warmth getting stronger as we passed through the wooden gates. The rain was still falling hard, and a cold wind was bending the trees around the farmhouse. I couldn't make out any clear patterns, any unusual combinations; although there was a mist hanging low to the ground, and healthy plants starting to come out in the garden earlier than expected. But the numbers hid out, slippery, shady, hard to identify and understand; there could have been a string, a formula holding all of them together in a way that escaped me; but mostly, it just seemed like they didn't even try.

Inside the farmhouse, Dante and Bea were holding hands, sitting in front of the fire. The farmer I had spotted with my binoculars was there too, tidying up the kitchen. We immediately felt each other as different and he looked at me suspiciously. But Dante came and hugged me, and the farmer lowered his icy eyes.

"So, what's up?" I asked cheerfully, joining them on the couch.

Dante and Bea started unraveling their story, talking at the same time, finishing each other's sentences. I listened carefully, but mostly watched the strange equations hanging in the room, especially above an old icon on the wall. Dante's problems were deep, but I didn't see a bad ending; I actually saw the lines of his future, smooth and lucky; he was going to be okay and happy, and live a very long life, and learn how to help others.

"I don't know if I can help you," I said when he finished. "I never met your father."

"You don't even believe that he exists," the farmer blurted out suddenly.

"Shut up, Peter," Saccas said loudly. "The girl is here to help. She doesn't have to believe."

"He can't be found by a *dmk*," the farmer continued, anger taking over his voice.

I knew the old Aramaic word. A chill went down my spine. How could he tell I was not part of this world, that I was not supposed to be there.

Saccas took the farmer by the shoulders and into another room. "He's crazy," Dante whispered to me, winking. "He told me my Dad is the man in that old icon. But that's an image of Jesus."

"Ah," I said. "Okay then."

Around the room, the numbers started to smell of lavender; for the first time they made sense, aligning in what was obvious from the beginning, only I could not see it. Somehow, I was in the presence of the divine; of the mysteries that had escaped me for so long. God wasn't there in that moment, but I could see that He had been there many times, traces of his moonlight steps all around; I peeked at the icon and saw a tender face looking back at me, ready to forgive me for sins I could not recall. I viscerally refused its generosity, still stubborn, and yet it didn't turn away from me.

The mystery of Dante's past was now solved; his genuine kindness and naiveté, his ability to ignite love at first sight in men and women alike.

I got up and walked to the next room, where Saccas was whispering to the farmer; they looked up at me.

"Would he have what I'm looking for?" I asked directly. "If you think that he does, then I'll help you find him."

"What are you looking for?" Saccas asked.

"I need to breed," I said simply. "I can't let my gifts and my knowledge disappear with me."

"Forgive her, God," the farmer prayed passionately, his eyes raised to Heaven.

"We're still here on Earth, and you are stuck with me," I said. "I can help you, but can He help me?"

Saccas thought about it for a while. "He can fix anything, if that's what you're asking," he said finally.

"But He won't just do everything that we stupid people ask him to do," the farmer said. "You can't just ask Him to fix a broken shower. He's not your servant."

"I realize that," I said. "But I will find and save Him, and bring His son back to him. That should count for something. All I'm asking for is that He answers to one prayer."

"We can't guarantee anything," Saccas said. "His decisions are not ours to understand. But we can promise that we will put in a good word for you."

I knew he was not lying; he was incapable of it. "How about you, Peter?" I asked the farmer. "Are you on board with this?"

"It's an abnormality, a mistake," he complained.

"So was His marriage to Dante's mother," I answered dryly, "and maybe his whole decision to keep living here with us. We all make mistakes. He knows human flaws, he has a few himself since He is half human after all."

The farmer looked puzzled, then nodded. "If you find Him, I will be grateful to you, whatever you are," he said. "That's my promise."

"All right," I said. "Now we can all go back and start our investigation."

Back in the large kitchen, I sat down and took control of the room. "Everybody quiet down and let me concentrate," I said. "Does He really look like that icon?" I asked the farmer.

"Of course," the farmer said.

I closed my eyes and delved into the anamnesis; strong, icy and hot shivers crossed my veins, as I was pouring through billions of painful and happy memories. I was following a yellow path I had imagined for myself, across beaches and cities, forests and skyscrapers. His face was hovering above me, gently directing me, until I found a dead janitor from the Company. I stopped, confused. The janitor had died a year ago.

"Did you guys ever met a janitor named Jim Alba at the Company?" I asked Dante and Bea, who were looking at me fascinated.

"Are you talking to the dead?" Bea asked with a small voice.

"Yes," I answered, "yes, I am. Now, did any of you know Jim?"

"Jim is not dead," Dante said suddenly. "I know Jim, he was friends with Eric. We chat sometimes. He came into my cube just a few days ago, and we talked about why dust bunnies are called dust bunnies. He's very much alive."

"You must be confused, honey," Bea said. "I remember distinctly that Jim died last year because they brought him to me and he was in such bad shape, I had to call Dr. Maygny. Then I heard that he died. They had an investigation and everything. I was even invited to the funeral by his sister, whom I met when she came to the Company to pick up some paperwork."

"Okay, people," Dante threw his hands in the air. "I know Jim, and I know that he works every day from

6:00 AM to 12:00 PM, and he says he never missed a day of work in his life."

Saccas and I looked at our watches in the same time. It was 11:30 in the morning.

"Let's go," I told Saccas.

We left, just the two of us, after getting a description from Dante and Bea. Jim Alba was a very old Hispanic man with a slow and polite manner; he liked to light a cigarette every time he left the building after work, and smoke it in the back of the building. That's where we waited; at 12:00 PM sharp, Jim appeared. Saccas and I looked at each other. None of us had really believed Dante; after all, he had an imaginary friend named Eric.

"Jim?" I asked smiling, approaching him. "How are you?"

"Okay, dear, I'm okay," he said, trying to light his cigarette with shaky hands.

"Here, let me help you," I said. I held the lighter steady until he puffed the first smoke.

"So Jim," I said, "how are things back home in Xela?"

He looked surprised but smiled, like I brought up a good memory. He was probably used to chit-chat with employees all the time and figured I was simply one on his cleaning route.

"*Bien, bien*," he said. "All is good back home."

"Maria okay after that accident? How old is she now?" I asked, digging through the memories left behind by Jim Alba when he died.

He started to panic visibly. "Who are you, Miss?" he asked. "I don't remember telling you about my poor cousin Maria."

"Well, Jim," I said, "just tell me this: Am I crazy, or do I remember being at your funeral last year?"

He turned his back and started to walk away, but Saccas and I easily caught up with him. "Tell me what happened, Jim," I said. "I know you're dead, how come you're wandering around cleaning toilets?"

He didn't say anything, but drops of sweat appeared around his temples. "I'm not dead," he muttered. "I'm not dead. I died but they saved me."

"Who saved you, Jim?" I asked.

"The doctors," he said and pointed vaguely towards the Company's building.

"Which ones?" I asked. "Tell me their names, Jim, or I'll haunt you every day and every night."

"Please, Miss," he said. "It was Dr. Maygny, at the Institute across the street, 20th Floor," he said, and I let up following him.

"You know," he said turning back to me, "you don't have to haunt me. I have nightmares all night. They sweep me in, the dreams. They call me."

"That's because you belong there, Jim," I said. "I hope you get there soon. I'm sorry for your troubles."

He shrugged and left. "All right, Mr. Saccas," I said cheerfully, "we have a lead. What do you say?"

"You are truly gifted," he said, smiling. "I bet Dr. Maygny has the evil sign on his forehead; to bring up bodies from the Dead is to fight both Nature and God... Who knows what else he is up to. So, shall we go back to our hiding place and hatch a plan? I will try and make some phone calls, and come back at night when no civilians are around."

"You do that," I said. "I have to go home. My parents will die today. Call me later and tell me where and when to meet you tonight."

He looked at me, surprised yet again. "I'm sorry," he said.

"It's okay," I said. "They lived a very long time. Good-bye, Mr. Saccas."

"You can call me Paul," he said warmly, shaking my hand. "I will pray for them."

"Thank you," I said, and it felt like a small relief.

CANTO X

Ever since I can remember, there was something on the horizon that attracted me; sometimes I would catch a glimpse of it – a subtle mist, moving, changing shape with ease; it had no numbers anywhere near it; in fact, I saw it dissolving patterns and eating its way through established equations if it so pleased. I always knew that that was where I wanted to be; that that was where I was supposed to be; and if I went there, things in Nature would be balanced again, as they should be.

I had studied Death for a long time; I wrote scenarios and found temporary explanations, only to discover that there was more to it than I had thought. It was a natural law and so it could be bent ; however, everyone in my family had agreed that you could only fool it for a long time, but not make it disappear. I identified with Death many years ago; in a way, I was a part of it once, and was then mistakenly brought back to the other side; I almost remember that I was happy there. I sometimes think I was a free spirit there, flying around in cheerful circles, with no numbers to hold me down, and then my aunt worked out her spell, and they caught me and brought me back here, in this prison of flesh and pain. I was not meant to be alive; I did not fit anywhere, and my skin hurt and I missed the wings I think I used to have; I had betrayed Nature by learning how to survive it, by wanting love and babies of my own, and so Nature had corrected that and eliminated that risk when I was a young child. I had become human, and had human needs and duties to my family; but sometimes, at the horizon, the mist would call my name with such a powerful voice, I had to cover my ears and scream.

When I came out of my meditation that afternoon, my visions did not fade right away back into the anamnesis; the voices persisted longer, stronger, the random stories of people's lives kept repeating themselves to me. Even after death, people still thought their story was the most important that had ever happened; they were never bored of telling it over and over again, trying to share whatever little wisdom they had gained. I had to walk into the shower followed by foreign feelings and sounds, and shampoo my hair with my eyes open because I was afraid that if I closed them, I would also see the images accompanying the tales.

My parents' voices were not as strong as I had expected; they had come into my thoughts as I was meditating, simply, without a fuss. I felt their unbelievable love for me warming me from the inside, unconditionally, totally. Thirty five years ago, they wished for me from the bottoms of their hearts. They dreamed of me, a little baby girl, to give a form to their great love; to heal the hard lives they had, the mistakes they had been making , the bad hands they had been dealt. My mom was young, with big brown eyes and long, wavy hair that flowed down her back. My dad was simple and honest, and always helping someone. He was the one who fed and named all the stray animals, the one who took care of sheep and rabbits and cows and pigs at the farm. His dog, Rex, was so loved that he was part of the wedding ceremony. He loved kids and often stopped and played a game of soccer with them when he came home from working the land. My dad was strongly anchored in Nature, a lover and protector of life in all forms. My mom was fragile, with alabaster hands, and hid from the strong sun and farm smells. She was sick since childhood, but had learned how to avoid the pain and crises with spells and potions. Her favorite herb, a reddish grass that only grew on the Crucea Mountain, was the one that finally helped her get pregnant.

They met just before midnight in the garden; she had the plants in her hands, already prepared and wrapped in inscribed pieces of papers; the magic words, ready to roll from her tongue. He had a shovel, and proceeded to dig the mushy ground. My mom spread the herbs on he ground and they gathered the dirt feverishly to make a small doll; my mom took off her large wool shawl and covered the doll with it, and held it in her arms as you would hold a baby. Then they waited.

At midnight, an angel batted her wings over them. She sat on my dad's shoulder.

"Is this the child?" the angel asked softly.

"Yes," said my mom, shaking. "Please help her, she was very sick and died just a few hours ago. Please bring my baby back. She is just an innocent girl."

"Was she supposed to die?" the angel asked.

"No, no, she sure wasn't", said my mom, crying. "It was my mistake, I left her alone for a second and the evils got her."

The angel flew above them, gently. "Hold her closer", she said.

My mom held the doll close to her belly. When the angel spoke to the baby, my mom also spoke, in a rushed whisper, all the magic words she had prepared.

"Did it work?" asked the angel.

"No", said my mom, crying. "No, it didn't. I guess it was not meant to be."

But it had worked – the seed of life had been planted in her womb. She laughed and cried and embraced my father, as the angel flew back to the clouds. They carefully took the doll inside. Nine months later, after I was born, the doll was sent to America with a friend of the family. He stopped in Gaithersburg, Maryland and buried the doll in the woods around Clarksburg. He then continued to Florida and my family lost track of him, as they requested him to.

All the noise and emotions had been quelled by the time I had made the coffee; Lou was nowhere to be seen. I called and look around, but apparently he had decided to haunt some other place that morning. I shrugged and left the coffee maker on, in case he returned later. He liked the smell of coffee. I had to meet Saccas at the doctor's office to see if we could find any clues.

I started to feel the first tingle as I was getting into my car; my body immediately went into defense, localizing the unusual feeling to my right hand, under the nail of my thumb. I stopped and asserted the danger – because any strange sensation in my body was indicative of a breach of my carefully constructed armor, a sign of discomfort or disease that should not have been penetrating through to me. The tingle was small but tangible, and it seemed to pulse gently, growing just a bit stronger by the second. I turned around in a panic and checked the numbers on all surroundings, as far as I could see; but the numbers were numb and lifeless, and they didn't talk to me.

I was always capable of seeing a little into the future; it was easy to follow the patterns and guess where or how they would end up. People's problems only seemed complicated to themselves, but to me they appeared laid

out in worn-down braids I have seen over and over
again. Oftentimes the paths were clear and led to
inevitable dead ends, and yet people would walk on
them full of hope, blinded by fake signs and wrongly
placed faith. Even my own way was many times visible;
it had led me to America, and it had held its promises as
I followed it in a plane over the ocean.

But that evening I saw no future in front of me.

--*

I had thirty-two thousand eight hundred and fifty-one
heartbeats left to live when I parked near the Company's
building. I could literally feel life packing its bags, ready
to leave my body in a few hours. I stepped out of the car,
expecting to be panicked or hurried; but instead I found
myself very calm and even oddly relieved.

Saccas's car was there too, and he came towards me.
Dante and Bea were following him.

"Why did you bring them?" I asked Saccas. "This might
be dangerous."

"I couldn't keep Dante away from saving his dad,"
Saccas said smiling. "And I couldn't keep Bea away
from Dante."

"You know, Anna," Dante said to me, "it's like I don't even know you anymore. Why are you acting like my boss? We used to drink coffee together and laugh at stupid people."

"I'm sorry," I said. "I don't have a lot of time. Let's go."

The Institute for DNA Sciences, across the street from the Company's Gaithersburg offices, was a mysterious building. Dante and I once commented how we never saw any people going in or out of it; everyone had to use the underground garage. Bea had never been there either; her instructions were to call Dr. Maygny if there was an important case at the Company, but she had never met him in person.

The building was empty and quiet, which we expected to find at night. We carefully went around the building until we found one of the back entrances. Saccas produced a badge from his pocket. The lock blinked open, much to Bea and Dante's enchantment.

"We have many friends," Saccas explained to me.

"I bet you do," I said.

We rode the elevator in an eerie silence. Dr. Maygny's office was clearly marked up front once we got out on the 20th floor. Saccas's badge worked its magic again and the door opened wide in front of us. We stepped inside carefully. It was a large office made of several rooms; nobody was there.

"What now?" Dante asked.

"Okay," I said. "Dante and Bea, find some records or something, see if you find your dad's name anywhere. Paul, let's look around."

We walked into every room, including the two bathrooms, but couldn't see anything except the usual machines and instruments you find in any medical office. We turned back to the entry hall, where Dante and Bea were leafing through papers.

"Nothing," I said. "You?"

"These are not real records," Bea said. "I don't know these names, nobody here is an employee at the Company. I thought the doctors here were supposed to take care of our employees only. And look at these procedures, I don't even know what they mean. Surgery in Operating Room 4? There shouldn't be operating rooms around here, this is not a hospital."

"Maybe there are other records somewhere?" Dante asked.

"Look some more," I told them. "Let's try and find these Operating Rooms," I told Saccas. "We have to look for the rooms behind the rooms."

"Everything okay?" Saccas asked me gently.

"I'm running out of time," I said. "We have to hurry, I don't have long. Poke the walls, see if they sound different."

We found the second door only after I observed the slight inaccuracy in numbers; they formed a lock code where there wasn't supposed to be one. The door was hidden by a wall of climbing plants; they shivered and pulled off when I came close.

Inside we found a small room with a bed and a sink; on the bed, a man was lying down, his hands and feet tied with heavy spells. He seemed sick and his eyes were closed.

"Oh, Father," Saccas shouted, falling to his knees.

"Wait," I said. The numbers trembled and moved; alarms were sounding somewhere, I could feel it. "Let me make a path first."

The spells were like hungry wolves wearing down their prey; they had a mind of their own, and piercing eyes to stare Him down. They were black and dense and moved fast, like evil does.

It took four minutes to start untying the knots of the numbers they used; to see through the mirrors and tricks they used. I slowly pushed and moved until the numbers aligned in harmless strings around us, pulsating, waiting.

"We should hurry," I told Saccas. "The way I figure, the alarm already sounded, and the path might close soon. Get him out now."

"I'll go get Dante," I told Saccas, but he was too busy freeing the man and didn't reply.

When I turned, I saw Dante already in the doorway, eyes wide open, tears streaming down his face. Bea came from behind him and immediately ran to the bed.

"He hasn't eaten or drunk anything in a long time," she said, checking the man's pulse. "He is extremely weak."

"We're going home, Father," Saccas whispered. "We're going home now."

And he lifted the man in his arms with infinite tenderness, and we rushed out, before the spells closed back behind us.

--*

Christian was still unconscious when we got back to the farm; Saccas had carried him in his arms to the car, and Bea was trying to revive him the best she could. He finally opened his eyes as they were passing through the gates; I was following them in my car. The rain had stopped and, for the first time in months, the night sky was full of stars. As I drove in, I thought I saw a luminous pattern under the oak trees; it shined through in the moonlight as if it was winking at me; but I didn't stop – it somehow didn't seem so important anymore.

The farmer and Saccas helped Christian inside and laid him down on the couch. The house smelled of lilacs. The farmer had prepared a hot drink and he immediately started to feed it to him; Christian drank slowly, color coming back in his cheeks. He looked around and smiled at us, and we all felt happy. He signaled to Dante to come closer, and hugged him with all his might.

"Dad..," Dante started, but Christian put a finger at his lips. There will be enough time to catch up, to explain. He then bowed towards Saccas and the farmer, silently acknowledging their help. He looked at Bea with love and acceptance, and gestured in her direction as if to bless her.

Then he turned to me.

"So you finally found me," he said weakly. "I was hoping you would."

I didn't answer; I had many things to accuse him of, a lot of anger to air, but that was not important anymore. I had less than a few hours left to live.

"Make your prayer," he said. "I will listen."

As I was preparing to formulate my wish, I saw the scene for what it was; a family and friends, reunited; what makes life bearable, the part of us that is good and expects no rewards in return. I saw myself for what I was, a body and soul, good and bad, young and old, tender and tough; I saw that nothing about my life was my fault, or anybody else's fault; that the walls I had built around me were made of lies and fears, and that it could have been much simpler if only I had known what to believe.

Suddenly, it felt unimportant to leave my genes living in this world; it felt selfish to think that I had to continue, that the world would suffer if I were to go. I understood that there were others like me, that I was unique but no more unique than anybody else. My family had tapped into ancient powers, and we had become ancient and obsolete as well; we only gained personal pain and discomfort; there was no greater good that came out of it. We lived selfishly trying to take things that weren't rightfully ours, and carved our time out of other's. I could see now how we were wrong; how we needed to be eliminated, silenced. I could see how we stood in the way of other patterns being created, other numbers painted in the sky of humanity, other ways discovered and wondered upon.

So when I prayed, silently, I asked for forgiveness for all of them: my mom and dad, my aunts and uncle, my grandparents; I asked if we could meet again, on the other side, and start anew, and live well. I prayed for the human race, for our humanity to always win; for food and water and warmth for everyone; for puppies and deer and elephants running happy and free; for friendly, lost ghosts to find their way home; for the numbers to be there to guide us towards our better choices; for Nature to be gentle with all of us.

I raised my eyes to him and smiled; he bowed his head.

I bowed back.

"I am going now," I told the others. "My old friend Lou is expecting me on the other side. I bet he has some tea and cookies waiting. And my family will be there too; I can't wait to see them again."

I hugged Dante and Bea, who didn't understand what was going on.

"I'll see you Tuesday at Wings & Claw," Dante said cheerfully.

I shook hands with Peter and Paul, and once again smiled towards Christian.

"I know you now, so you will forever live in me," Christian said. "Go in peace. You will be happy there."

"Thank you," I said.

By the time I was at the door, they were already talking about Monday's meeting; I knew that they would be okay, that they would be there and take control, and make everything all right again with the Company and the world. They had won once more, in yet another battle with the dark side of our souls; and I was happy to have helped them.

On my way out, I stopped under the oak trees and picked up the entanglement of long grass and fallen tree branches which clearly spelled 2-2-9. I cried as I let it fall back to the ground; I had nothing to ask of it anymore.

--*

It was dawn and the sun was shining already as I drove up I-270 towards Frederick. I didn't know where I was going, or if it mattered; but I wanted to be away from the city and into Nature, to make it easy for it to take me. I was ready to give up the battle and surrender to the peaceful mist in the horizon; I felt liberated and light as a feather.

From I-270 I took a two-lane road as I approached Clarksburg; there were no other cars but mine. I drove slowly and looked at the horse farms around me, and the beautiful houses, and the amazing forest. When I saw a dirt road, I turned right and drove on it until it dead-ended on top of a hill. That was a good place to die, I thought. I parked on the grass and got out of the car; I could see the city of Clarksburg in the distance, beyond the small patches of trees.

I had nine heartbeats left when I heard the truck revving its engine. It could have been waiting for me there, or maybe it had just been summoned then. The numbers around me signaled danger and death, and rushed my blood to my heart; but I didn't move. I lovingly thought of Feliks and what could have been, but I let go; as the numbers froze around me, trapping me with the grip of death, my last thought was of a bigger love; my fingers created patterns of joy and forgiveness as I fell down, to be left there in the woods for other people to find. I used my last breath to inspire my spirit into the equations around me, for the future poets to pick up when the breeze gently bent the grass.

As my body sank into the wet ground, Nature finally accepted it and caressed it; roots pulled it in and surrounded it with their warmth; the flowers under my nails grew out and smiled to the sun, golden. My body melted into the dust it had come from, never to be seen again.

I found myself back home, hovering freely over the mountains of my childhood. In the Delta there was a picnic and the smell of grilled *mici* filled my senses; my Dad waved at me; everyone else was there with him, drowned in light and brightness. I flew down happily, laughing.

THE END